The Light In His Darkness

A Maple Small Town Romance Series
Book 2

Copyright © 2024 Jessica Whaley.
All Rights Reserved.

Cover Design © 2024 Jessica Whaley

Editing by Pat Norton

Jessica Whaley
P.O. Box. 785
Leesburg, Al. 35983
authorjdwhaley@gmail.com

ISBN: 979-8-9906151-2-0 (Ebook)
ISBN: 979-8-9906151-3-7 (Paperback)

Dedication:

For those who deserve their own second chance.

A Note to My Readers:

This book was written in a time that I was healing through a lot of traumas in my life; most specifically, our miscarriage.

I want my readers to know there may be certain triggers within this book and your mental health should always come first. It is okay to DNF a book if it becomes too much for you. This is still a small-town romance with a HEA.

While this story does have a happily ever after...some parts of it is dark. Derek, the MMC, shows his pain and his baggage deeply. His point of view is things I thought when going through the trenches of our miscarriage and other things in my life.

Writing this story was my second chance. I hope it can show you that you are worthy of second chances too.

Possible Triggers within these pages as follows:
Nightmares

Infant loss:(This does not pertain to the MFC, however it is discussed and it is apart of the story.)

Loss of spouse: does not pertain to MFC

Mental abuse: such as going back and forth with anger.

This book contains explicit adult scenes and languages.

It hits on depression: such as not cleaning the house, etc.

I trust that you know your triggers before continuing to read this book.

Xoxo- Jess

Prologue
13 years ago
Rodeo Fair Grounds, Texas.
Megan

"Got everything you need, spud?" My grandfather asks coming around the corner of the horse trailer.

I nod, not able to say anything as I try to shake off the nerves. This run is the biggest of my barrel racer career. If I can secure any of the top 5 spots on the leader board, my name is automatically qualified for the NFR. The National Finals Rodeo is a big deal. Only the best of the best in the world qualifies for the opportunity to compete there in Vegas. I would be one of the youngest in history just to have my name on the NFR roster at just 14 years old.

We made the drive all the way out to Texas for me to run tonight. Just my grandfather and I. Collin, my little brother, stayed home with our grandmother to help her with the farm while we were gone. Right now, I'd give anything to be back on the farm with them. My nerves are getting the best of me.

Molly, my trusted and go-to partner, stands tied to the trailer as I start to saddle her up. The arena lights are bright around us and the crowd cheers from the stands. I grab the cream-colored saddle pad from the back tack quarters of the trailer after brushing Molly's body off. She and I warmed up as soon as we got here earlier so she should be ready to go.

Throwing my saddle over her back, Molly's ears shoot up. "Ready to run, girl?" I ask her and, as she always does, she licks her lips, replying to me.

I smile. I love this horse more than she will ever know. She is a young filly my grandfather bought specifically for the farm, but I fell in love with her and trained her on the barrel pattern myself. She loved it. I hope she always does. After cinching up my girth, I grab the breast collar around her front breast and click it to the saddle. The rhinestone in the front is sparkling in the lights.

"Make sure you allow her the reins in between barrels," my grandfather says after watching me tack up. He is one of my biggest supporters and the father figure in my life since my parents died years ago.

I nod, "Yes and ride with seat and legs, not my hands." I smile at him, and he smirks back, pride beaming over him. "She knows her job, Megan. You both make a great team even if you did take her from me," he jokes.

I laugh. "It was meant to be."

The stands roar as the calf ropers get done with their event and the announcer transitions everything over for the barrel racers. My grandfather gives me a hug like he always does before a run. I mount Molly and pat her neck. It was time to show the world what we were made of. We have practiced so much back at home, it was time to show them we belong at the professional level.

Molly prances under me and it makes me a little more relaxed. Feeling this animal under you, who could kill you, but you both work together as a team; it is the most humbling feeling.

"Let's go girl." I grab a hand full of her mane brushing my hands through it before sitting up tall. Squeezing her sides with my legs, I urge her to walk toward the arena, my grandfather not far behind us.

The crowd roars as we get close and the barrel racers are all starting to gather around in the holding area waiting for their names to be called.

A few riders go before us and they all make clean and careful runs. The ground was not looking so good after a few runs and the tractors make their way out smoothing the dirt back out. My grandfather's hand goes to my knee. "Just have fun, spud. You were made for this life." He grins at me.

I smile back at him. "Thanks grandpa. Thank you for allowing me to do what I love."

"Next up is a cowgirl who is no stranger to the game. She comes from a long line of ranchers and farmers and we are happy to have her tonight. When you're ready, Megan Mapleson," the announcer says over the loudspeakers and my heart races.

"You got this, Meg!" my grandfather says backing away from Molly and I nothing but a big smile across his proud face.

I smile at him and take my reins in my hands, leading Molly to the arena alleyway. She prances under me, knowing her job is about to begin. She rocks back and forth and I giggle a little as I pat her neck. "Let's do this girl…"

The adrenaline pumps through me as we head to the first barrel. I sit down in my seat grabbing my saddle horn and Molly turns it without a second thought. I give her reins as we go to the second, sit back in my seat again as we turn, and then the world goes black.

I can hear the crowd gasp as I open my eyes slowly and hear footsteps running towards me.

I'm laying on the hard ground.

My head hurts.

Molly is laying down beside me, she isn't moving.

I slowly get up and make my way to her head. "Molly!! No, no. Don't be hurt. Open your eyes girl!"

My grandfather's hand goes to my shoulder. "Megan, are you okay?" He looks over me. "You need to not move, let the medics check you out."

"I don't care about me. Molly needs help. Her leg!" I scream and tears flow down my face.

"It looks broken," an older man who came to help says.

"No!! It can't be!" I scream holding her neck in my arms.

"You are okay girl. You are going to be okay." I rock back and forth holding her head in my lap. She doesn't fight me. The weight of her head eases into my lap.

"Jeffrey, might be best if we put her out of her misery," one of them said to my grandfather.

He nods and looks at me, tears streaming down my face, "Megan, she's not going to be able to race anymore. It's broken. She may never walk again."

"I don't care if she never races again. She's my best friend. You cannot do this to me or her. I will never forgive you." I give him a stern look.

The crowd around us is silent. It feels like the air thickens.

"How much would it be to transport her to the nearest equine vet like this?" he asks one of the men standing around.

My eyes perk up. "You think we can save the leg?" I ask him full of hope.

He bends down next to me and his eyes glisten with tears. "If there is anything I know for certain, my Megan can make anything happen when she believes it will hard enough."

I smile and hug him. "Thank you, grandfather."

Chapter One
Megan

BANG. BANG.

"Megan!" I'm jolted awake from my dream and look around in a daze...

BANG. The noise runs through the trailer again. Adjusting my eyes, I realize where I am and what is going on. The knock on the door of the horse trailer living quarters rocks the loft I'm sleeping in.

"Your horses won't feed themselves." Camryn's voice calls from the outside and I groan, grabbing my phone and checking the time. Shit.

I've overslept and my chores still must be done. That dream felt so real, and my heart is still pounding in my chest. I look down at the tear stain on my pillow. It was like I was back there, in that arena seeing him and hearing my grandfather's voice. It was almost like he was giving me a little pep talk before my run tonight. I grab my jeans I left laying across the couch last night and pull on a grey tank top I found out of my stack of clean clothes. Quickly brushing my teeth and throwing my long dirty blonde hair up in a messy bun, I pull my boots on and run out the door, almost falling as I step off the last step.

"Oh, don't give me that look," I say sarcastically at Crackerjack as he sticks his tongue out at me. I keep him in a round pen by the trailer at night, so he doesn't have to sleep on the back of the trailer where it is cramped. Grabbing the feed buckets I leave hanging over the fence of his pen, I walk to the fairgrounds to fill them up with water.

It is the last rodeo of this circuit and I'm in the running for some big money and qualifications. I have been on the road all year and have not been home to see my family for most of it. When my grandparents died, my cousin and brother, along with my cousin's husband, decided we wanted to continue their legacy they had left us, the farm, and our breeding program.

I get to continue my dream by riding our young horses in the rodeo circuit for potential sale. Right now, though, it's just me and Crackerjack and he will never be sold. He has been one of my favorites since he was born.

"Here you go sweet boy," I tell Crackerjack as I pour his feed and water into their own buckets on his side of the panels and rub his forehead. His long dark tail swishes, getting flies off his backside.

I watch him in admiration. He has grown so much and has turned into the most beautiful red roan gelding I have ever laid eyes on, although I was there when he was born so I may be a bit biased. He is now seven years old and one of the biggest blessings in my life.

We are in Tennessee this weekend at the Buckle Bunny Rodeo grounds. A few of the Markell sisters bought this land a few years ago and have marketed it as one of the biggest rodeos of the year for our circuit. Cowboys and cowgirls from all over the United States are entered every year to earn a spot at being professionals.

Trailers and trucks line the back of the arena where the contestants stay. Some bring their own golf carts to ride around so they don't have to unhook from their trailers. Most of us are in the same circuit and get used to seeing each other every year.

"Meg," Camryn, another cowgirl in the circuit who I have made friends with, comes over to my trailer. "I'm running to town to grab some drinks. Do you mind watching my trailer while I'm gone?" she asks me.

"No problem!" I reply. "Here, let me grab you some cash if you don't mind grabbing me a few things too while you are out." I run in the trailer to grab a few dollars from my purse and hand them to her. "Just a few dr peppers and a deli sandwich of some kind. Thanks Cam," I tell her as she walks to her truck.

It's a beautiful sunny day out and I open the canopy on the trailer so Crackerjack has shade to get under where the sun doesn't tire him out before our run tonight. Pulling my lounge chair out and putting it under the canopy too, I take out my Kindle and start reading one of my dark romance books that I bought last night at dinner with the restaurant's Wi-Fi.

***

I can hear the crowd roar as the stands fill with people from all over waiting to watch the show. Standing at my trailer, I'm dressed in boot cut jeans, a bright pink button up, and a rhinestone cowgirl hat to match. My hair flows down my back straight as I could get it as I put my cowgirl hat on my head and walk over to Crackerjack who is standing tied at the trailer, saddled and ready to go. His saddle pad and the boots on his feet are both bright pink to match me.

"Welcome Folks to the 7th Annual Buckle Bunny Tennessee Rodeo!" I hear the announcer come over the loudspeaker as the lights cut on and music starts. I take a deep breath and grab Crackerjack's bridle from the panels I hung them on. He paws at the ground, getting impatient with me and I chuckle.

"Alright Mr. Cocky Britches." I put the bridle around his ears and take the snaffle bit, guiding it into his mouth. "Let's keep that energy locked up until we make our run." I pat him on the neck and his ears pop up toward the sounds of the arena.

"Ready to go?" Camryn says passing by me with her paint mare. They are both decked out in teal colors. She stops to wait on me. Grabbing ahold of the reins I placed around Crackerjack's neck; I pull myself up on my saddle and place my feet in the stirrups.

"Let's do this," I reply to Camryn and walk with her toward the arena with the other riders heading to the grand opening.

The grand entrance for a rodeo is a big deal. We also have a prayer, a tribute to our military, and respect to the America we all love. The whole reason for the rodeo life is to show people who are not from this way of life what America used to be. It's a way to show how man and animal working together for a common purpose is what the American way was founded on. It was my grandfather's favorite part and I remember him always removing his hat and standing for the whole thing. He was an army veteran, and I am so proud of the sacrifices he made for us.

Getting to the front gate, we all line up behind the flag women who lead us in. The announcer asks everyone to bow their heads and all of us with hats on take them off, placing them over our hearts as he says a prayer. Then, the National Anthem plays. We all stay still other than a few of us whose horses prance under them. The crowd stands in respect and quietness. Then, suddenly, "American Soldier" by Toby Keith starts playing and the leader of the flags, The American Flag, goes out as the song plays followed by the rest of the flags. We follow behind them, lining up around the panels throughout the arena.

"These cowboys and cowgirls are from all over…," the announcer starts, "showing us what can be done when man and animal trust one another…," as the song ends and the girls with the flags exit. The announcer's voice disappears from my focus as I put all my effort into keeping Crackerjack calm coming out of the arena. He always thinks just because he is in an arena he should be running. We all exit behind the cowgirls with the flags and the crowd claps for us as we ride by.

I take Crackerjack back to the trailer while the first event starts- the calf ropers. I can hear the crowd hooting and hollering and some laughs from the rodeo clown doing his job. I grab a bucket with water and let Crackerjack drink as much as he wants.

My phone rings and I notice it's my cousin, Maggie. "What's up Mags?" I ask, sitting down for a minute.

"Just wanted to let you know we are heading to the hospital! It's time." I can hear her breathing heavily into the phone and Logan's voice is saying something in the background I can't fully make into a sentence.

"Logan, we don't need all of that. Just get in the car," I hear Maggie say to her husband. I laugh. Typical Logan to be freaking out right now.

"Oh, Maggie. I will be heading home soon as tonight's run is over," I squeal into the phone. "Keep me updated!" I holler into the phone.

"I'm more worried about Logan than I am me." She laughs. "Good luck. Give CJ a kiss from me for good luck!" she says into the phone, then the line disconnects.

Maggie always said Crackerjack was too long of a name, so she nicknamed him CJ, and it stuck. She is more like a sister to me than anything else. It was just a few years ago I invited her over to help us around the farm and then as fate would have it, she is my long-lost cousin.

After a little while, I hear the announcer end the calf roping event and I grab my bridle to put back on CJ. Running my hands in his mane, he paws at the ground like he knows what we are going to do.

"Let's give them a show, Buddy." I rub my hand over his nose and pull up over my saddle, securing my legs into the stirrups.

We trot over to the warm-up pen that's on the back side of the main arena. A few other barrel racers are doing the same thing I came down to do, warm up the horses so their muscles are ready for the tight turns we will be doing. I nudge CJ's sides with my spurs, and he starts loping; listening to my pressure, I give in to his sides and the small pull in the reins putting him into a circle pattern eventually expanding into a figure eight. We do a few figure eights on both sides until I feel like he is warmed up enough.

"Let's get ready for some barrel racing!" The announcer says and a few staff members take barrels, lining them up in the correct four-leaf clover pattern. I pull crackerjack to a stop, and he prances under me not wanting to slow down. We walk over to the arena where the holding pen is, waiting on the announcer to call our name to run. The tractor finishes plowing the dirt and goes back up to where it sits during events.

"I think I was a tenth away from your time last night," Camryn says, walking her mare up beside me in the holding pen. I laugh and CJ's tail flicks at flies on his back.

"I'm going to miss you during the off season." I give her a smile.

"Me too, sister. Hopefully I will see you in Vegas. Stay in touch if I don't see you leave out." She gives me another smile.

We watch a few barrel racers go before us and make clean runs. My nerves hitch up and my heart rate speeds up as Crackerjack sways under me.

"This cowgirl coming up is no rookie to our circuit. She's a cowgirl not just in the rodeo arena, but also at home on her family ranch. She can keep up with the best of them. Hoping to secure her right to be at the National Finals Rodeo this year, let's see if she has what it takes tonight." Music starts playing and I hear the crowd roar. "Get on your feet and cheer her on folks. Let's go Megan Mapleson!"

I swear Crackerjack knows exactly the name that was announced; his ears perk up and his feet under me prance fiercely. I smile at the familiar feeling and rub his neck, "You and me buddy. Let's make some dust."

As we get close to the alleyway, CJ rocks under me. I try my best to hold him back until we get to the spot before the alley opens in the arena. He rears up slightly and I laugh at his eagerness. His power is something I will never get over.

He makes his way up the middle of the alley and as we make it to the end, I give slack in my reins and put pressure into his sides, giving him the okay to open his stride. We make our way to the first barrel, the money barrel. Leaning into the butt of my saddle, I let CJ flow around it, and it was perfect. Grabbing my saddle horn, I lean up as we go between the first and second barrel, I sit as he flows around it so easily. Pulling myself back up and on to the third, I kick just a little to push him to go faster and sit back as he turns the third. Placing my reins on his neck and let him have all control as I sit up coming out of the third heading to the alley.

"New leader!" The announcer says as we pass the timers, "With a time of 16.12." The crowd roars and I pull Crackerjack into a small circle slowing him down and patting his neck.

"Thank you boy," I tell him, and he prances with happiness rocking his head. I smirk at the cocky personality this horse has been given.

Now, let's go home.

Chapter Two
Megan

It is just half past six in the morning as I enter Maple city limits. I loaded Crackerjack up early this morning after getting a few hours of sleep then loaded up the rest of our gear and headed home. The rodeo circuit is over for the springtime, so I have a few months to enjoy being home with my family.

The WELCOME TO MAPLE sign comes into view and I smile at the familiarity. My family are the original founders of the town, and everyone here takes care of each other. Passing by the stores on Main Street, I see Nana's diner. It was my grandmother's and when she and my grandfather passed a few years ago, it was left to my cousin, Maggie, and I. She runs it more now since I have been gone, but I'm back now to help as much as I can.

Ring, Ring.

An incoming call comes through on the Bluetooth of the truck, "Hello?" I answer.

"Where the hell are you?" My brother Collin's voice comes over the speakers of the truck. I roll my eyes at his annoyance. He is four years younger than me but since coming into his manhood, he likes to think he's the keeper of me, not the other way around. I was the one who basically raised him and I won't let him forget it either.

"I just entered Maple," I answer.

BANG.

Oh. My. God.

"Collin, I got to go, I just got hit in the side of the horse trailer." I hear him holler on the other end but hang up before figuring out what he was saying.

I put the truck in park and jump out, looking over the trailer, and check through the window on Crackerjack. Thankfully, he is okay.

Running around the trailer to the side where the other car is, I notice an elderly man stepping out of his old white sedan in dark color pants and a light color t-shirt. He looks terrified. My first instinct was to lay into him, but I pause. He also looks confused. My heart pulls at me, he reminds me a lot of my grandfather when he was having an Alzheimer's episode.

"Oh, miss. I am so sorry. I got turned around," the elderly man says with a shaky breath. He looks around nervously. "I didn't hurt your animal, did I?" He looks like he is having a tough time getting a deep breath.

"No sir, my horse is just fine," I reassure him with a light smile.

By now, bystanders are crowding the area and sirens from the nearby fire department are heard in the distance. I roll my eyes at the nosy people.

"Meg! Are you okay?" A few people ask me, and I nod my head, yeah. But I notice no one knows this man. He seems to not be from here.

"Sir," I ask him as I place my hand on his arm, "Where are you from?" He looks up at me with uncertainty. Looking at his car and back at me he replies, "I-I don't know."

"Everyone okay?" A male's voice comes up beside me and I jump.

"Yeah, we are okay." I glance at the man who looks to be with the local fire department in fire gear.

"He doesn't know where he is at. He seems very confused." I look back at the fireman, "I don't want a report done. My trailer is fine, my horse is fine. I need to get home, and he needs to be cared for."

The fireman, who I might add does not look much older than me, is just standing there obviously assessing the entire situation. His brown hair and tanned skin make him the epitome of bad boy and his deep ocean blue eyes scream trouble. He is covered in his turnout gear holding his helmet by his side. He also is looking very grumpy now at me.

"We are required to do a report, and why don't you let me take care of him and you just sit there and answer questions for the police." He walks past me to the older gentleman.

"You must be new here." I say to him sternly and he stops in his tracks turning to me.

"Why do you think that?" he asks with a huff.

I smile. "Because you would know who I am and that my family is the whole reason this town exists if you weren't new here." I pause gathering my words. "But since you don't have any manners, I won't use mine either. The police know where I live. They can find me there. I have a horse who needs off this trailer and family who are waiting to see me at home." Not giving him another chance to reply I turn to the old gentleman and smile, "You are going to be okay. This grumpy fireman is going to make sure you get back home to your family." I pat his hand and cock an eye at the grumpy guy in fire gear. He just stares at me with a pissed-off look.

Turning to walk back to my truck, I climb inside and grab my phone. Shit. Collin has called me at least twenty times. I hit his name to call him back.

"You cannot tell me you have been in a wreck and then hang up!" Collin says as soon as he hears my voice. "I was about to head toward town and look for you!" He sounds out of breath.

I laugh. "I'm okay. CJ is okay. We are about to turn on the driveway now." My brother and I have always fought like cats and dogs, but I know he always has my back when needed.

"I'll meet you in the barn to help you unload. Then we can head to the hospital together." I smile at the thought as the line disconnects. My two best friends in the whole wide world had a mini version of themselves last night and I cannot wait to meet the little guy or girl. They voted to keep the gender a secret until birth. I opposed the decision, but I was obviously outnumbered.

Our MAGNOLIA FARM sign hangs at the entrance of the driveway, and I smile at the thought of my grandparents. They loved this farm with every fiber of their being, and we vowed to keep their legacy alive after they passed. The sun is shining over the grass that sparkles with dew from the morning mist. Horses and cattle share a pasture along the driveway, and some are grazing in the field while others stand at the bale of hay, eating.

Coming around the curve, the farmhouse I grew up in comes into view with the big Magnolia tree beside it. It still looks the same as it always has. Big porch with a swing on the front and our dogs, Reba, Izzy, and George, all sit up as they see me arrive. Reba is the alpha and the best damn livestock guard dog we have ever had. She is getting older now and it makes me sad to think we may not have her for much longer.

Izzy and George are our two blue and red heelers. I named them from my favorite tv show, Grey's Anatomy, when we brought them home as puppies. They learned from Reba and have really stepped up in protecting the animals.

I pull the horse trailer down to the barn and the dogs leap off the front porch to come meet me. "Hey guys!" I run to them, kneeling and letting them attack me with kisses.

"Yeah, yeah. We are all happy she's home," Collin says coming out of the barn and walking to the back of the trailer. I groan at his crankiness. I know he is secretly happy I'm back home, too. Collin opens the trailer door and unhooks the latch door that keeps Crackerjack safely inside.

"Come on big guy," Collin says while grabbing CJ's halter and walking him backwards off the trailer. "I got water and feed in your stall ready for you."

I smile at the thoughtfulness.

Collin walks CJ into the barn and I unload the buckets and gear into the tack room, making a mental note to myself once we get back that I need to clean it all up. Molly sticks her head out of her stall when I walk out of the tack room. I give her a smile and make my way over to her, rubbing her nose as she nudges me.

"I know, girl." I run my hands through her mane. "I'm happy to be home too. I wish you could have gone with me." I kiss her nose and walk over to CJ's stall, checking to make sure he's all good while I'm gone.

"Ready?" Collin says walking out of the stall and latching it shut. "They are waiting for us."

I smile.

"Do you know the gender yet?" I ask him.

He shakes his head no. "They wanted to tell us together."

I grin with excitement while we walk out to Collin's truck to head to the hospital.

***

Maple is such a small town that the nearest hospital is a town over near the nursing home. It's not a level one trauma center or anything but it handles pretty much anything us cowboys and cowgirls throw at them, including baby deliveries.

Stepping off the elevator on the labor and delivery floor, Collin and I make our way to the front desk to ask the nurse where to go.

"She is in room three-twenty." She points in the direction of the hall we need to go down and then adds, "She has been expecting you both." She smiles and goes back to her charting.

I laugh. Leave it to Maggie to have everyone watching for our arrival. Reaching the door to their room, I knock and hear Logan say, "Come in!" I slowly open the door as Collin follows behind me.

Logan basically runs to me, wrapping me in a hug. "Meg!" He shakes us in our hug, and I chuckle. "Maggie made me swear I wouldn't tell a soul the gender until you two got to know." He backs up from our hug, wrapping his arms around Collin's shoulders.

I look over at the bed and see Maggie sitting up on pillows, an IV stuck in her arm and holding a little wrapped up burrito in her arms. Tears prick my eyes and I smile up at the cousin who is more like a sister. She has tears in her eyes, too.

"God, I've missed you!" Maggie says to me, and I wrap my arms around her. She hugs me back. "And this," Maggie says as we pull out of our hug and she pulls the blanket back from the infant's face, "Is Rhett Landon Parker." She smiles up at me and tears stroll down both of our faces. Landon was our grandfather and my uncle, her dad's, middle name.

"Oh my gosh, guys!" Collin says as his voice breaks. He hugs Logan.

"Do you want to hold him?" Maggie asks me and I can't form any words; all I do is hold my hands out, nodding like a lunatic.

I hold Rhett steady in my arms, being mindful to support his head, and I look at his perfect little face. If he's anything like his mom and dad, he will be strong. His little lips poke out and his eyes open just a little.

I love him so much already.

Chapter Three
Derek

The beeping coming from the fire trucks as we back into the bay of the fire hall is all I can hear until we turn the engines off. I jump out and start taking my turnout bottoms off and hanging them up on the back wall we keep them on. My blood is still boiling from the wreck we were just out on. An elderly man hit a woman driving a horse trailer and he was confused. The amount of nosy people in this town is ridiculous, too. They all wanted to make sure the woman and her horse were okay. The audacity that woman had to speak to me in such a way. I could have easily had her arrested for not respecting us and the scene. To say she got under my skin is an understatement.

The other guys leave out in their trucks, but I decide to walk into the kitchen of our lounge area first to grab a drink. I open the fridge harder than I meant to and take a bottled water from it.

"Heard you had a run in with a Mapleson." I jump when I hear the deep tone of the man behind me. A man I respect more than anyone and who was there on the darkest day of my life.

I take a deep breath as I turn to face Captain Miller. He slides on top of the bar stool across from me at the bar, looking amused at my anger.

"That bitch has it coming next time I run into her," I snap at him, shocking myself at how clipped my tone is. I do not understand how this woman could have me this unhinged.

In an instant, his smirk is gone and he is on his feet in front of me. "Listen here, boy. The Mapleson family are the whole reason our beautiful town exists. They are some of the best people around. Megan has been through a lot in her life, and she has a lot on her plate. You will treat her with kindness when you are representing our department. Do you understand me?" The look on his face tells me I don't have an option either way.

Pushing my luck, I huff, "She needs to learn how to respect emergency personnel."

He shakes his head. "Derek, I know you are new here. You have been through a lot yourself, I know. I get it; but Megan and her family are some of the best people you will ever meet. I would advise you not to get on her bad side. That family would give you the shirt off their back if you needed it. Even if it meant they did without. Did you help the man who hit her?"

I nod, "Yes sir. EMS was taking him to the closest hospital, and we contacted his family. He is a dementia patient. He had a bracelet on his arm with numbers to contact."

"Good." Captain Miller says, "See, she's a good woman. I heard she was more worried about him than herself. Take my advice, let it go. You will be glad you did."

As the last words come out of his mouth, he exits the room, leaving me alone with my thoughts.

I down the rest of my water and try to take a deep breath.

I know I am new here. I just started in this department a few weeks ago so I do not know this town like everyone else and that is exactly what I wanted. A new fresh start after the hell I have been through. I do have a lot of respect for Captain Miller. He was there on the day I lost everything that meant something to me. The day I wish I died. The day that still haunts my dreams. He held me up when I did not want to keep living. He offered me a change of life when he invited me to live in Maple and apply to be a firefighter for his department. So, for that, I can respect his authority here, even when I do not agree.

As I walk back out to my white Dodge Ram, I look around at the beautiful town before me. It's the epitome of small-town USA. The kind of small towns country music hits are created from. If the Mapleson family founded this little slice of heaven, I can only imagine the kind of people they are. I hope they all are not as ruthless and opinionated as Megan.

I have a new job lined up next week and for once, I finally feel like life is turning around. I needed this; a fresh start. How I wish I could go back to the past and change things. The guilt that I carry is unimaginable. It was my fault. All of it. I am the reason my life is the way it is now, and it fucking hurts.

Pulling my truck out of the parking lot, I decide I want some lunch before I go back to the room I have been renting at the Magnolia Inn. This is the last week I will be staying there. This new job is going to allow me room and board for working and I am anxious to see what this new place and life is all going to be about.

I will miss working as a paramedic. It was my dream job growing up, but I needed to get away. The nightmares are bad enough; I didn't need the hell I'm living through to set me on fire every day I go into work. The triggers happen without warning, being in the same spaces that brought me the worst day of my life. I still enjoy helping people, but I am cautious about what I allow myself to see now.

Megan comes back to my mind as I pull into Nana's Diner. It has become one of my favorite places to eat. I try to shrug the feeling of how beautiful Megan was, and her ability to not give a fuck and stand her ground when it mattered was mesmerizing. No matter how much of a bitch she was this morning, another part of me wanted to know more about her.

I shake my head; no, you are not ready for that.

And I don't know if I ever will be.

How do I even share my past with someone else?

How do I tell them what I did?

It was all my fault.

Too much of it consumes me.

Its baggage I don't want to give to anyone else.

That would be selfish of me.

My mind goes back to her blonde hair and her beautiful green eyes.

My dick stirs and I must readjust it before I get out to go inside the diner.

"You don't get to make the decisions around here," I say to my cock as I open my truck door.

Chapter Four
Megan

A week has passed since I've been home and I'm so happy being back on the farm. Being back in the home that raised my brother and me is everything I have been looking forward to. I miss smelling grandma's cooking as I walk through the doors. I was a little shocked at how the place still looked the same as when I left six or so months ago. I hadn't expected Collin to decorate much since I've been gone, but he has kept everything the exact same.

Logan and Maggie decided they would take a trip to visit her father for a few weeks with Rhett. Her parents got a divorce a few years ago and she does not have anything to do with her adoptive mother anymore. Her father, James, is still regularly active in her life and to hear her talk, he is over the moon excited about being a grandfather.

"Meg," Collin says as he walks in the door of the house while I'm going over reports for the month at the kitchen table, "want to go to Hilltop tonight?" He grabs a water from the fridge.

I set down the papers I'm looking at and chuckle, "You mean to tell me that place is still busy?"

He laughs, taking a sip of his water, "You know us small town folks don't like change in our town."

I grin. He's right. If I've learned anything from our small town, it is that these people are loyal to their own. They make sure we are all taken care of.

"Sure," I answer my brother. "When do you want to go?" I ask him.

He looks at the clock on the wall. "Give me an hour to shower and change, I smell like horse shit." He runs upstairs to the bathroom, and I laugh.

＊

We decided to take Collin's truck to Hilltop, and it feels like old times again. My brother may be a big pain in my ass, but I know I can always count on him. I decided not to change too much and chose to keep my boot cut jeans and boots on. I only changed out of my T-shirt and put a hot pink crop top tank on. My loose curls flow down my back.

As we pull out of the driveway, "Dust on the Bottle" by David Lee Murphy is playing on the truck radio. Collin reaches over to the volume dial and turns it up and we both sing along. Maple is still the same as always as we drive along main street toward Hilltop. Nana's Diner, the one Maggie and I co-own together, it was our grandmother's, is flourishing. I have been so proud that Maggie has left it just the way grandma had it.

Hilltop is covered with trucks and cars in the parking lot and lights flicker inside. Collin finds a tight parking space near the back that the truck barely fits in. I open the truck door holding it tight, so I do not hit the truck beside us since I did not have much space to work with.

"Geez," I start, "I think this place has gotten busier since I left."

Collin meets me behind the truck, and we start walking toward the front door. "Yeah, we had some new young people show up here looking for work. They all like to hang out here on the weekends and some weeknights too." He holds the front door of the bar open for me to walk in.

I'm hit with the familiar smell of cigars and some of the best food around. The place has not changed a bit. Familiar faces come into view, and they all tell me hey or hug me as I pass them.

It feels good to be home.

Making my way over to the bar across the dance floor, I see the bartender is not behind it. I sit at a barstool waiting on his return. Collin walks off with a group of his friends to the pool table and I take in the scenery.

"Did you get that report done?" a male's voice says behind me, and I jump nearly out of my skin.

Turning to look at him I can't do anything but stare.

The firefighter.

Holy shit, he's HOT. I could not tell much from him at the wreck since he had his fire gear on but both arms and neck is covered in black and white tattoo, and his right hand has a skull tattoo on it. His dark brown hair is cut short but what gets me most of all is his eyes. Those deep blue eyes are staring at me like they are thinking sinful things.

I gulp. "I told you I didn't want a report done."

I start to turn away from him, but he stops me with his hand on the stool near my thigh. My body start to betray me while a fire heats up in my core.

"I told you that you didn't have an option," he snarls at me. The fire in my core is nonexistent now. I instantly remember why I do not like him.

He removes his hand just in-time for me to jump off the stool and poke my finger into his chest. His eyes look shocked for a brief second, but his snarl is back faster than it was gone.

"Let's get one thing clear, pretty boy," I start, "I don't care who you are, you will not talk to me that way." I don't break eye contact with him and by this time I can feel everyone's eyes on us.

"Everything okay over here?" Collin comes into my view with his group of guy friends. They think they need to protect me, but I can take care of this prick myself.

"It's fine, Collin." I wave him off. "Mr., I'm sorry I didn't get your name." I look at him for an answer.

"Derek." He replies in a short tone.

"Mr. Firefighter Derek was just going to leave me the hell alone before I kick his ass." My gaze never leaves his. His nostrils flare.

"Derek Murphy?" Collin asks, and I roll my eyes.

"Collin," I huff, "Go away now."

Collin pulls my hand down and steps in front of me and Derek. "You are the one who saved our barn a few weeks ago?" Derek nods but his gaze doesn't leave mine. Eventually Collin puts his hand out for Derek to shake.

I look up at Collin. "What happened to our barn?"

Derek finally looks Collin's way and shakes his hand.

"We didn't want to worry you, Meg," he runs his hands through his hair, "but our hay loft caught fire a few weeks ago. Derek and his crew were first on scene. Logan and I couldn't get it out fast enough ourselves." He pauses, "Derek saved Molly. A bale of hay fell through the loft right into her stall. He jumped in after her and got her out. She could have died." He looks at me nervously afraid of how I'm going to react. "We put new wood up before you came home so you wouldn't ask questions. We knew if you heard about it, you would have dropped out of the rodeo circuit and come straight home."

I take a deep breath and look at Derek, "Thank you for saving my old girl, but you are still on my shit list."

"That's Megan's way of giving a compliment," Collin informs Derek.

He nods slightly, understanding.

I roll my eyes. "No, it's my way of being thankful for him saving the horse that means a lot to me but that I still don't consider him a friend." I stare at Derek.

"Let me guess, you are going to be my new boss?" Derek looks between me and Collin. My head snaps fast up at Collin who is running his hand through his hair again.

"What the hell is he talking about?" I ask Collin who looks like he wants to be anywhere else right now.

"A few weeks before you came home, Maggie knew she and Logan would be gone for a while visiting her parents, so we decided it was a good idea to hire some seasonal help." He grins at me sarcastically.

I drop my head on the bar, and I huff.

"Yes," I look up at Derek, "Unfortunately I'm going to be your boss."

"When is it okay for me to move in? I knew I was supposed to start work tomorrow," Derek asks.

"You can move in tomorrow morning," Collin says, and I grab his shirt pulling him into me.

"Move in where?" I ask him annoyed.

"The house?" He half smiles nervously.

I drill my eyes into my brother with a look of disgust.

All the idiot would do is grin back, obviously enjoying this.

Taking a deep breath, I turn toward Derek, pointing my finger at him again, and he takes a slight step back. "You listen, and you listen good. I don't take it easy on anyone. You will be at the house at seven sharp in the morning. We start chores at seven on the dot. Come ready to work your ass off." After the last word, I stomp off toward the restroom to get away from all of them.

"Is she always like this?" I hear Derek ask Collin.

"You have no idea what fun you are in for." Collin pats him on the back and they both turn back to the bar.

I now want to go the hell home.

Chapter Five
Derek

Hilltop has become one of my favorite places to relax since moving to Maple. It is an effective way to release the tension of some days and, mostly, the nightmares.

The bar is full tonight. The smell of cigar smoke lingers throughout the building. Town folk of all ages hanging out, dancing on the dance floor, and at the bar ordering drinks.

She took my breath away as soon as I saw her enter the building. If you googled,

COUNTRY GIRL, I'm a thousand percent certain a picture of Megan Mapleson would come up. She's beautiful enough to be a city girl but she is dangerous enough you know she's all Southern woman. And everyone seems to love her, which pisses me off.

I cannot be jealous.

Watching guys walk up to her, hug her, and smile at her makes me want to cut off their hands, or jerk out their eyeballs if they do it again.

What the fuck is wrong with me?

She's danger with a capital D, but right now the wrong kind of D wants her attention.

My dick twitches.

Down boy.

The way she walked my way tonight, not realizing she was walking toward me made me want to wrap my skull tatted hand around her throat and pull her lips to mine.

My dick twitches again.

What the hell is wrong with me?

I haven't been riled up like this since…my past.

The past that still haunts my dreams and steals any ounce of joy I will ever have.

And now to find out I have to spend every day with the woman who makes me act like a hormonal teenager who just figured out how to whack it... abort mission.

I might as well just sign my soul over to the devil himself because I am fucked.

"Don't worry man. She has her moments, but not all of them are bad." A guy who was standing in Collin's friend group says with a grin, "She is a badass and knows what it takes to survive."

I nod, "How do you know her?"

The guy smiles. "Who doesn't know Meg around here? Her and Collin's grandparents were some of the best people in this town. The family made this town what it is. We all went to school together, rode horses together, and got into trouble together growing up." He hits Collin on the back, "Isn't that right brother?"

Collin laughs. "He's right, Derek. My sister helped raise me. She's a good person, just territorial. Her motto is tough love."

I nod again as the bartender sits my beer down in front of me.

A blonde and a brunette walk up to Collin. The blonde puts her hand on Collin's shoulder but its not until her eyes meet mine that I suddenly feel sick.

She gives me a soft smile. I can tell she suddenly feels uncomfortable seeing me, too.

I take a huge chug of my beer and before I know it, over half of it is gone.

"Dang man," Collin says, noticing my beer.

"I'm going to go," I tell him, standing up and putting cash on the bar for the bartender.

"Oh, come on. There's someone I want you to meet," he states pulling the blonde closer to him.

But I don't want to meet her. I already know who she is. That day, the worst day of my life, comes into view.

"I guess Megan left," Collin says oblivious to my fight or flight body language.

The blonde stares at me with eyes that I know. The same eyes she had. Eyes that make me remember so much I wish I could forget.

I feel nauseated.

"I need to go man," I tell Collin. "Got to be at work early." I grin at him, and he nods, thankfully not pressing the issue.

I make my way away from them and out to my truck. She is the last person I wanted to see tonight or ever. I jump inside my truck and put my head on the steering wheel trying to calm my breathing.

The nightmare that consumes me comes rushing. I can hear the screams, I can feel the tears, I can remember it like it happened yesterday.

I need to get drunk.

But not here.

Not in front of her.

Driving out of the parking lot, I drive to the nearest gas station and pull out my phone to call a buddy.

Maybe he will let me drink away my sorrows and sleep on his couch.

***

I pull up at Levi's fifteen minutes later and he's standing on the porch waiting on me. I sigh, I can read the look of concern all over his face. He's one of my old friends from working on the ambulance as a paramedic. We went to EMT school together and he has been there though every big aspect of my life—good and bad. I knew if I was okay with anyone seeing me like this, it was going to be him.

"Hey buddy," Levi says as I jump out of my truck with a case of beer in hand. "What is going on?"

I huff, not really caring for the questions and the pep talk I am sure is coming. "I saw her."

Levi looks frozen for a minute. "You saw who?"

"Her. The one who is supposed to stay far away from me. I made it clear the last time I saw her or her family that I didn't want anything to do with them."

"Derek, man. I'm sorry. I know you have had it rough, but so have they. You can't expect to live this close to their town and not see her. If you wanted that much of a fresh start, you should have moved farther away," Levi states.

"And leave you?" I joke. "Never."

He chuckles, "You know my couch is always available to you, but once Crystal moves in, I don't know how she will feel about it."

I snap my head up at him. "You proposed?" I ask.

He nods. "Two days ago. Sorry man, I was going to tell you but just thought it was too soon for you to hear about something like that."

I can't believe it; one of my good friends is getting married. Who would have thought that day would come. An uneasy feeling hits me—he is moving on. Eventually everyone will move on and leave me to deal with my hell by myself. I will eventually be all alone with the devil himself. I deserve it. I deserve every bit of it.

I laugh shaking off the feeling in my gut. "I get it."

Levi opens the door to the house and we walk inside. "Where is she tonight?" I ask him.

"Work. So it's just us tonight." He grabs my case of beer and throws it on the counter. "So how about we have a boys' night like old times." He smiles and opens the case of beer.

"I knew I called the right guy." I take a beer out and pop the top.

"So," Levi starts, "met any new people in Maple?"

I huff, "Just one infuriating one. Her name's Megan Mapleson and I am afraid she is going to be a pain in my ass."

Levi laughs, "Megan's tough. Good family though; you need to stay on her good side."

I roll my eyes.
Great. My friends even like her.

Chapter Six
Megan

A little after seven the next morning and Derek has not shown up yet.

Strike one.

There is so much to get done today and not having an extra hand puts us even more behind. I grab a soda from the fridge and head to the front door to meet Collin at the barn. As soon as I make it out on the front porch, Reba starts barking at the driveway. A white Dodge is making its way to the house faster than it should be with dust flying behind it. The truck parks right beside my black Chevy and the driver's door slowly opens.

"My alarm didn't wake me up," Derek says slowly getting out and shutting his driver's door. Jesus, he sounds hungover.

I huff stepping off the front porch and toward him. "Maybe next time you won't get drunk the night before you start a new job." I look down at his bag. It is small for someone who is moving in for a few months.

I eye him carefully, "You travel light."

He looks at me with a glare. "Not much need to travel with things that don't matter anyways," he says vaguely, and I dismiss the thought of asking what he meant by that.

"Throw your bag inside the front door and follow me to the barn," I tell him.

"I don't get breakfast before work?" he grunts.

"You are a grown man who should have gotten here in time to eat." I pause. "There might be crackers or something in the fridge in the barn." I turn to walk away. I hear Derek throw his bag inside the front door and he jogs back to me.

"So, what's on the agenda today, boss?" He asks me as we walk into the barn. I look around for Collin, but he is not anywhere to be seen.

Grabbing a shovel from the tack room and throwing it in the wheelbarrow in the hall of the barn. I gesture to it.

"Your first chore is mucking stalls." I give him an evil grin. Derek looks back at me and the wheelbarrow.

"You are shitting me, right?" he asks with a growl.

I turn my back grabbing a halter from the tack room and walk over to Crackerjack's stall.

"No," I pause, "One thing you will learn about me is I mean what I say. Get to work."

Dereks feet seem to be frozen in place, but I choose to ignore him as I walk into CJ's stall and wrap the halter around him. Once I lead him out to be tied for me to saddle him up, I notice Derek still has not taken a single step.

I huff. "What is the matter now?" I ask him.

"It's just, I thought I would be doing bigger work than mucking stalls. This seems like kid work," he snarls finishing his sentence.

Before I realize what I am doing, my nose is almost touching his and my finger is pointing at him like last night. "Let's get one thing clear, no one is above anyone else here. We all pull our weight. These animals help us do many things and deserve to be taken care of." I turn on my heels back to CJ.

"If you did not sound like an entitled little brat maybe I wouldn't give you kid chores," I state sarcastically.

We are both silent for a moment and then a thought crosses my mind. Without looking at him I ask, "Why do you need this job anyway? Aren't you a firefighter?" The saddle in my hands flew effortlessly threw the air as I toss it onto Cj's back.

Derek is quiet for a moment, not wanting to answer my question. He takes the wheelbarrow to the stall CJ came out of and starts mucking.

I guide the bit into CJ's mouth before mounting his back. Placing my foot in my left stirrup, I pull myself up and throw my legs over CJ and I feel Derek look up a me.

"The fire department is just volunteer. They don't pay, and I needed a job. I met your cousin, Maggie, one day at Nana's and she had a flier on the counter looking for some seasonal help." Derek goes back to shoveling.

"You mean you go into burning buildings to save literal strangers without pay? You put your life on the line because you volunteer to?" I ask him.

He is quiet but nods.

Wow. Impressive.

But he is still on my shit list.

I nudge Crackerjack's sides, asking him to walk on toward the arena. Looking around at the land before me, I still do not see Collin anywhere. Wherever he is, he needs to hurry the heck back home; there are horses that need exercise.

***

It is lunch time and I'm getting worried about Collin. He has not replied to any of my text or calls. I got all the horses ridden and Derek just finished mucking all the stalls. Making my way out of the tack room, putting the last bit of tack up for the day, I stop dead in my tracks and burst out laughing.

"I think the point is to put the shit in the wheelbarrow, not on your clothes," I snicker at Derek.

"You are hilarious," he answers sarcastically.

"Lunch is here!" I jump as Collin's voice enters the barn.

I turn quickly to face him and put my hands on my hips. "What the actual hell? I have been calling you!"

He shrugs. "Sorry, I got held up. But I brought us all some lunch."

I notice he is trying to hide his neck from me. Quickly walking up to him and grabbing his arm, I pull his chin so I can see his what he is hiding.

I gasp.

"COLLIN JEFFREY MAPLESON!" I yell at him. "I know that is not a hickey on your neck!!"

He pulls away from me quickly and runs his hand through his hair like he always does when he is nervous.

"Explain yourself now!" I yell at him.

"There was a girl at the bar last night." He smirks and I hear Derek take a deep breath.

"Did you know about this too? Why he was not here? And you did not tell me?" I snarl at Derek this time.

He throws his hands up in surrender. "So, Collin, what did you bring us to eat?"

"Lunch from Nana's," Collin says, smiling at me boyishly. He knows I can't resist the food from our grandmother's restaurant. I'm thankful she taught our cooks how to cook like her before she passed, but I still miss her meals lingering throughout the farmhouse.

I roll my eyes at the two children in front of me and walk past them toward the house snatching the to go bags from Collin ignoring his shit eating grin he always does when he knows he has won an argument. I take out my phone and text Maggie.

You left me here to baby sit two five-year-olds. When are you coming home? *Sad face*
P.S. Give Rhett loving from me.

My phone instantly dings.

Haha. I'll trade you a husband that acts two and a baby that wants to suck me dry all hours of the night.

I laugh out loud and instantly feel better about my situation.

On second thought, I'll keep the five-year-olds.

DING. I look at my phone.

I thought so. Be home sometime next week. I'm so tired of this place already. I want to be back on my little piece of heaven.

P.S. Sorry I didn't warn you about the new hire! Take it easy on him.

I hit LOVE on her text and pocket my phone with a laugh. Maggie knows me too well. As I get to the front porch, I hear footsteps behind me.

"So, was it the blonde or the brunette?" Derek asks Collin.

I roll my eyes.

I don't give Collin time to answer as I open the front door of the house turning to face them, "You both do me a favor and keep the pussy talk to yourself and away from me."

Collin nods, walking past me and I stop Derek before he gets by. "And one rule, no bringing them over here. If I find out you have a girl in your bed, I will fire you on the spot. Is that clear?"

He salutes me with a grin. "Yes boss."

Chapter Seven
Derek

I have always assumed I had a good work ethic. I was working a job the moment I turned sixteen but even before then, I was cutting grass for the neighbors or trying to find ways to make money. Going through EMT school was not easy and I worked a lot of times in the most unsafe positions and long hours. Being on this farm has made me feel like the laziest son of a you know what. Megan and Collin can work circles around me in a heartbeat. Throwing hay, mucking stalls, throwing, and picking things up that weigh twice or three times their size and it never ends. They might stop for a second getting a drink of water but then they are on to the next thing that needs to be done. I always heard farm kids are a different breed, and I'm seeing it firsthand.

Collin and I tried to distance ourselves from Megan for the afternoon. She did not seem to be in the mood for our man jokes. She told us there was a fence in the back pasture that she needed us to take a look at.

"Is your sister always so cranky?" I ask Collin as we drive off in the red Polaris Ranger to check and fix some fences.

Magnolia Farm is gigantic, and it takes all my breath away looking at the beautiful creation laid out before me. Natural creeks, the largest trees and grassy fields with horses grazing. We cross a small creek, and I grab the handle at the top of the Ranger as we go over to steady myself. Coming up the hill, horses are spread out before us grazing. I blink rapidly a few times so my eyes and brain could catch up to one another. The scenery before me looked like something from a painting, yet I was seeing it right before my eyes.

"She is not so bad once you get to know her. She is just a believer of tough love like I said last night. In her eyes, if you are easy to run off, you are not worth putting the time or effort into," Collin says driving us over a bigger creek.

I nod but stay silent while the water splashes on both sides of the Ranger's wheels.

I can feel Collin smirking at me, and he finally says, "I see the way you look at her, man. Tread lightly. She is not some girl you get in bed and shove her out. It takes a lot to get her heart, but once you have it, you have it for life. Trust and words mean a lot to her. She watched our grandparents go through so much, and they were still holding hands in the end. That is the kind of love she wants and deserves." I can hear the tension in his tone toward me on that last line.

"I'm not looking for that type of commitment," I finally reply. "Plus, I do not look at her in any type of way."

Collin chuckles, "Whatever you say man. Just tread lightly."

He stops the Ranger as we get up to a fence that looks like it could fall over any moment. Collin puts his phone in the holder under the steering wheel and then grabs some thick gloves out of the box on the back of the tailgate and throws them at me then puts his own pair on. He grabs a hammer from a toolbox that is strapped down on the tailgate too. It is loaded down with any equipment we would need to fix anything while we are out here.

As Collin unloads the extra wood post and wire, his words linger in my head.

I do not look at her any type of way.

"Come hold this post for me, Derek," Collin orders and I do as I am told.

"Never thought I would be working on a farm some day," I chuckled.

Collin pulls the loose wire around the post silently but after a moment he replies, "Never thought I'd meet someone who could rival my sister or tried to." He grins.

I roll my eyes, "I do not rival her."

Collin ignores my eye roll. "Whatever you say, man. All I know is no one ever questions her or tries to defy her. For some reason, you get under her skin easier than I do and that says a lot." He shakes his head with a laugh.

Collin lifts his hammer to hammer the post, and I hold it steady. After a moment, I decide to change the subject out of curiosity. "So, what about that hickey?"

Collin grins. "I'm not sure what you are talking about."

He stretches the lower barbed wire tight and wraps it around the bottom of the post.

"Was it the blonde?" I ask nonchalantly, shocking myself for even bringing her up.

Why do I still care?

He looks up at me with a smirk, "Do you know her?"

I am gut punched as I muster up enough movement to shake my head no.

I used to.

She is a part of the past that haunts me.

"Man, she is the most genuine, laid-back girl I have ever met. She has been hurt bad in the past. Said her family has been through a tragedy and she is just now getting back into the dating world. Though she said she has an ex that will not leave her alone." He pauses, "Don't tell my sister, but I have been staying with her some because she does not feel safe at her place at night. He has tried to break in a time or two." His nostrils flare but calm down. Shaking his head he says, "Why she chose me, I won't ever know, but you best damn well know I'm going to do whatever I can to keep her happy." Collin's voice is full of hope and happiness.

No matter how far I try to run from it, the past still haunts me. I am the reason she has been through trauma. It is all my fault.

I watch as Collin hammers the remaining part of the fence up, a branch snaps to our right, getting our attention.

At first, I do not see anything but another stick snaps and my heart rate skyrockets.

My eyes widen when I notice the whites of the eyes staring back at us. And neither of us have our guns. The moment my eyes latch on to it, Collin notices it too.

"Do you see it?" I whisper to Collin, trying hard not to move a muscle.

"Shit. My gun is in the truck back at the barn," Collin says with a muffled voice. The eyes are slowly making their way closer to us as it creeps forward.

"Think we can make it to the Ranger?" I ask him.

"I'm not going down without a fight," he replies.

I nod, understanding we do not have a choice if we want to make it out alive.

I'm the closest to the Ranger and Collin is closest to the eyes that are stuck on us.

"Whatever happens, Derek, get to Megan," Collin says in a mumble.

I stay silent. The adrenaline starts to take over.

"On 3," Collin states.

"One…," I start.

"Two…," Collin whispers.

"Three!!" We say in unison and take off toward the Ranger.

As soon as I get to the passenger seat, I notice the Ranger did not dip beside me. My eyes widen and my heart rate accelerates even more as I look in front of me. I see the bobcat has jumped on Collin's leg and has tackled him to the ground. Collin is screaming out in pain, and I freeze, not knowing what to do. Suddenly, I notice his hammer is laying on the ground, and I rush to grab it and run to the bobcat, swinging the hammer. "Go away!" I yell as I swing the hammer back and forth toward it.

The cat backs off from Collin gradually and hisses at me but finally decides to run off.

Red is all over the ground and all over Collin.

"AHHHH!!" he screams out in pain.

"Call Megan!!" He screams at me, and I remember he put his phone in the ranger cup holder when we first got here.

My fight or flight starts to take over.

Chapter Eight
Megan

The sun is starting to go down and the sky looks vibrant with colors of orange and red as the sun is setting behind the mountains. After lunch today, we all got back out to work. Collin took Derek with him to finish some pasture fence work, but I'm pretty sure it was just an excuse for them both to get away from me. They should both be heading back soon.

I'm filling up the horse's water for the night and making sure they all have hay. Molly sticks her head out of her stall window to greet me and

I rub her nose, "My old girl, I sure do love you." She sticks her tongue out at me in response.

I feel my phone vibrate in my back pocket; quickly noticing it is Collin.

"What do you want now?" I huff into the phone as I balance it with my neck while I fill up Molly's water.

"MEGAN!" I hear Derek holler on the other end, and I drop the water hose on the ground. My heart rate spikes, and my hands start to shake. By the sound of his tone, something is wrong.

"Derek, what's wrong? Where is Collin?" I'm frozen in the hall of the barn waiting for a reply.

"I don't know how you will get to us. We are across a big creek in the back pasture. We are back near some woods with the Ranger. A bobcat ambushed us. It got Collin on the leg. I ran it off, but he is bleeding bad. I cannot get him out myself. I must hold pressure, or he will bleed out." Derek's tone is panicked.

I run to turn the water hose off and jump on our four-wheeler that sits in the hall of the barn and head off into the pasture they left out into earlier.

"Which creek are you at?" I yell at Derek over the noise of the four-wheeler.

"I don't know. It's getting dark. I can't really tell. It's a deep one. Pasture is full of horses. I saw a white farmhouse below the hill when we came in. There was a pond by it." He sounds out of breath.

Taking deep breaths, I try to calm down. That is Maggie's house he saw. I know the creek he is talking about.

"I'm coming. I know where you are. Keep my brother alive, Derek!" I yell into the phone.

"I'm trying! Hurry!!" His tone is full of fear, but I hear Collin mumbling to Derek on the other side of the phone.

"Tell her I love her," Collin grunts.

I close my eyes shut to keep tears from flowing.

"Megan, get off the phone with me and call 911." Derek's voice now sounds stern.

"Okay." I whisper. Hanging up quickly, I dial 911 as I make my way up the hill to the creek and press the phone as tight to my ear as I can so I can ear over the four wheeler's engine and crossing the water.

Dispatch: "911, what is your emergency?"

Megan: "Yes, m-my name is M-Megan. My brother has just been…" I pause to catch my breath, "attacked on our farm by a bobcat. He's bleeding out. I need help fast!"

Dispatch: "Ma'am, what is the address of your location?"

Megan: "Send them to my farm, Magnolia Farm in Maple. We are in the back side of the pasture on top of the big hill on the left from the white farmhouse. There's a gate right by the barn that will lead them up to it. They will have to cross a big creek to get to us. My farm help is with him. He's a firefighter for our local fire department, too. Im on my way to them now."

Dispatcher: "This isn't Megan Mapleson, is it?"

Megan: "Yes, ma'am, it is."

I hear the dispatcher gasp and she starts typing fast on her end on what sounds like a computer.

Dispatcher: "Oh honey, I'm dispatching everyone. Relaying this information to them now. Tell your farm help to keep your brother where they are. My guys are on their way now."

I take a deep breath, thankful for the people in our town. The four-wheeler gets out of the creek fully and I see Derek off in the distance. My heart stops when I notice Collin laying on the ground, lifeless. There is blood all over him.

"I tried to carry him as far as I could," Derek says exhaustedly. I notice he took he ripped some of his shirt off to make a tourniquet for Collin's leg. The bobcat got him right over the top of his thigh. The shirt and Collin's pants are soaked in blood. Tears flow down my cheek at the sight of my brother before me.

I kneel to Collin's level and say, "You don't get to leave me today. Do you hear me?" I pause and then whisper, "You, me, and Maggie are supposed to do this together."

I wipe a tear quickly, so Collin does not see it.

He barely opens his eyes, but his hoarse voice says, "You keep this place going. I love you." He barely squeezes my hand before letting go.

"Collin?" I look over him and his eyes roll back in his head.

"Megan, back away," Derek says sternly at me, "His heart just stopped."

I gasp and watch as in one swift movement Derek starts CPR on my brother. It's rough and I can hear ribs breaking. Tears flow down my face, and it feels like hours pass before emergency crews are all around us even though I know it's only a few minutes.

It feels like there are fifty people or more around me. Emergency lights are flashing everywhere, but my only focus is on the pale face of my brother. I have lost so many people in this life that mean so much to me.

Please God, do not take him, too.

They load Collin up on the stretcher and Derek stops CPR when they hook him up to a device that does it for him.

"Where are you taking him?" I ask the paramedic that is pushing drugs into my brother.

"The closest place that can stabilize him. We are going to Grace Memorial. You can meet us there." And in that moment, he does not give me another look. His focus is completely on my brother.

"Come on!" Derek says, grabbing me, and I fight him.

"No! I'm not leaving him!" I yell at Derek, trying to get out of his arms.

"Megan, stop!" Derek turns me to face him, and his face is serious, "You must let them help Collin. You will only be in the way. Jason is a great paramedic. He will do everything he can. Let's go and we can meet them there." He does not give me time to respond as I watch the paramedics put my brother in the back of the ambulance and fly down our driveway with lights and sirens.

Derek jumps in the driver's seat of the Ranger, and I get in quickly beside him. He floors it to the barn where he parks in the hallway, and we run to his truck following closely behind the ambulance.

***

When we pull up to the emergency room parking lot, Derek does not have time to put his trust into park fully before I am jumping out of the passenger side. I run through the front doors to the receptionist desk but there is no one there.

I pound my fist on it trying to get someone's attention. Derek's hand goes to my shoulder making me jump.

"Come on," he says, pulling me out to the doors of the entrance and over to the ambulance bay. The door to go in is locked by a code. Derek looks around making sure we are alone and then types in the code. The red light on the box turns green and he opens the door. I stare at him for a moment in shock and then run past him into the hall.

"Megan!!" A familiar face comes around the corner of the nurse's desk and I almost fall to my knees.

"Becky!" She grabs me to hold me up steady.

Becky was the nurse who took care of my grandparents in the nursing home. I have not seen her since they passed.

"When did you start working here?" I ask her while wiping a tear.

"Just a few months ago." She wipes another tear from my eye. "We got him back." She smiles at me while cupping my cheeks, and tears fill her eyes.

My wide eyes snap up at her and the tears flow even more.

"Where is he?" I ask her looking around at all the rooms.

She takes a deep breath, "He's in surgery. They have to close the leg up. But his vitals were stable for what his body has been through."

I nod, trying to control my tears of relief.

I feel a hand rub my back and I jump at the touch. Im a little embarrassed that I had forgot Derek was still standing with me.

"Let's go sit down and maybe get you some coffee?" He suggests to me in a soft tone, and he looks at Becky. "How about we keep the fact that I know the ambulance door code just between us."

She laughs, "I been telling them they need to change it." She pauses, "Take care of my girl." She squeezes my hand and Derek nods.

I follow him into the waiting area and we both sit down. The waiting room is small and plain Jane. The walls are cream and the dark brown chairs look like they wouldn't be comfortable to sit in for more than five minutes.

"Here you go," Becky says, walking in with two cups of coffee and some muffins.

We both thank her.

She starts to turn to walk away but first says, "I'll come get you when I know something." She smiles at me, and I nod.

I am just thankful he is alive.

Chapter Nine
Derek

Megan and I sit in the waiting room in silence. The television and the occasional sips we take of our cups of coffee Becky brought us is the only sound in the entire room. I do not think either of has the stomach to eat the muffins she brought. Looking around, I realize the room we are in; the room that I got the worst news of my life. The place I lost it all with a matter of a few short words.

I know what I need to do but doing it will trigger so much in me. Plus, I am not even sure if I still have her number.

I need to face my demons.

It is not just about me right now.

Pulling out my phone, I run through my contacts until I get to her name.

She has most likely blocked my number by now. I know I would have if it was me.

Collin really likes her. He would want her to know.

Typing out the text, I hit send and pocket my phone.

"If you got somewhere to be, you don't have to sit here with me." Megan's short tone mumbles beside me.

I pause for a moment, suddenly angry that she would think she could do this alone.

She shouldn't have to do anything alone.

"I don't have any plans. I can stay as long as you need me to," I reassure her.

She smirks, "I'm sure you have a hot date tonight. Isn't that who you were just texting?"

Not quite.

Then a thought makes me grin, is she jealous?

"I was pretty sure I was told to keep the pussy talk to myself," I joke trying to ease the mood.

Her mouth drops wide open at my smart-ass remark, and the image does something to me. I feel my dick twitch at the site. What I'd give for her to be on her knees in front of me and her mouth around my cock right now.

Well, maybe under different circumstances and not in a germ-infested hospital.

I shake my head trying to get the image out of my head before I look like an idiot with a boner sitting next to his boss.

"You know what I meant, asshole." She crosses her arms over her chest and turns her head.

I grin again. She's cute when she is mad.

Almost like a little sour patch kid.

I was about to say something else sarcastic when she stands and says, "I need to go call Maggie." And just like that, she walks out before I have time to respond.

Watching her turn the corner, I am oddly aware of how alone I am now in this room. The same room that haunts me. The room that I got the worst news of my life in. The room I told myself I would never be back in. But here I am, sitting with the woman that drives me insane in more than one way.

My phone dings. Pulling it out of my pocket, my brain reads the text repeatedly hoping it says something different each time, but it never changes.

I'm on my way.

My heart rate picks up as everything about that day comes into play. Her screams. Our cries. Me begging God to wake me up from the nightmare. Her hitting me in the chest as she screams at me. Her mother falling to her knees. Her father threatening to kill me. I can feel the room spinning and my hands growing sweaty.

The darkness is crowding me. The devil is laughing. He wants me stuck here. He wants me at his mercy.

I can't breathe.

I feel like a black hole is swallowing me and my vision is going blurry while darkness surrounds the edges. I grip the arm rest of the seat I'm in, but nothing helps. I'm spinning out of control with each breath.

"Are you okay?" Megan's voice comes into my ears, and I feel myself relax at the sound of her voice and my heart rate settle almost instantly. Everything comes back to focus as I focus on her. She calmed me before I could spiral out of control. No one has ever been able to do that before.

"Um," I rub my hand over the back of my neck, "Yeah, I-I'm fine. Just a little jittery from the coffee."

"Becky is moving us to a room. She said it is the room they will bring Collin to once he is out of surgery and recovery." She gestures to the hall cautiously looking me over like she does not believe my words. Thankfully, she does not question me, and she turns to walk out of the waiting room cautiously turning back before she is out of sight to make sure I'm following her.

I jump out of my chair and follow Megan down the hall.

Thank God he is going to be okay!

Chapter Ten
Megan

Other than the passing of my grandparents and waiting on Maggie to arrive to the nursing home, this has been the most anxious I have ever been. Riding and breaking young horses do not make me feel half this anxious. I think Derek can sense it because he has not said much to me since Becky left us alone.

We were moved into a hospital room after about an hour and a half of waiting and Becky assured me he was still alive, and someone would come to the room to update me as soon as they could.

So, we wait.

And wait.

And wait.

Derek turns the TV on, so some noise floods the room, but I do not even pay it any attention. With every footstep in the hall, I jump up to see if they are coming to our door.

But no one stops. They just keep walking.

Knock Knock.

After a while, I hear someone knock on the room door and I jump up to see who it is. The door slowly opens while I hold my breath hoping its someone to give me an update.

"Is this Collin Mapleson's room?" A small, framed girl with her blonde hair pulled into a ponytail comes into view. She is in blue jeans and a t-shirt, so I know she is not a nurse or hospital staff. Her eyes are puffy; she has been crying.

"Y-yes?" I say in a whisper.

Derek stands slowly as he notices her, "Alyssa?" he asks. My mind is slow processing, but I look at him and back at her.

She nods her head and tears fall from her eyes.

"Is he…is he alive?" she asks hoarsely.

Derek's body goes rigid.

"Yes, he's in surgery." I answer her unsure of why Derek is suddenly frozen in his place. Tears flow from Alyssas face as she sobs.

I roll my eyes at this bitch's theatrical act.

"And who are you exactly?" I ask sternly.

Derek finally moves and looks at me, "Megan, not now."

"I don't know who you think you are." I stare at Derek. "But that is my brother I almost lost today. MY BROTHER!" I yell at him. "I have a right to know why she's being so dramatic right now. If anyone has a right to be that way, it's me," I exclaim through tears.

Alyssa walks up to me. Holding her hand out, I notice she has a tattoo on her right wrist with the initials CM on it.

"Hey Megan, I've heard so much about you." She smiles holding back her sobs and holds her hand out to me. I just stare at it and back at her. "Collin and I have been dating for a few months now. I was supposed to meet you last night at Hilltop, but I was told you left early when I got there. I hate that we are meeting like this."

All I can do is stare at her. I've never known Collin to keep something like this from me. I know I give him hell, but this is something he should tell me.

"You can wait with us," I finally say, ignoring her hand and sitting back down.

"Okay then. Great," she says, taking a seat nearest to me. I roll my eyes.

Derek does not say anything while he takes a seat, too. I am glaring at him because by the looks of it, he knows more about my life than I do lately. I notice he stares at the floor, and his leg is shaking uncontrollably. Something about Alyssa makes him anxious. How does he know her? And who told her my brother was here?

"MEGAN!" I hear a familiar voice and see a familiar face run through the hospital room.

"Mags!!" I yell standing as fast as I can to get to Maggie.

"I came as soon as I got your message," she says wiping back tears. "How is he?"

"He's still in surgery, but the last update they said he was still stable," I tell her.

She nods but suddenly she notices we are not alone.

"Hello?" she says to our guest in the room. "You must be Derek. We haven't officially met but I'm the one who gave Collin the go ahead to hire you. I'm so glad I did!" She pauses and smiles, "Thank you for taking care of the two people who mean the most to me." Derek nods but stays quiet.

Maggie turns to Alyssa, "Are you his girlfriend?" She gestures to Derek.

They both say no in unison but are timid as they eye each other for a brief moment.

I snarl.

What is it with this girl?

Maggie looks at me confused.

I roll my eyes, "Maggie, this is Collin's girlfriend, Alyssa." I pause, "Alyssa, this is our cousin, Maggie. She owns the farm with us." I give a slight smile.

I watch Alyssa nervously stand and walk over to us, giving her hand to Maggie, "Nice to meet you, Maggie. Collin has told me a lot about you, too."

Maggie notices her tattoo and she stares at her and then back at me.

"At least you didn't know about this, too, or I would have been even more pissed," I say with a smirk and Maggie laughs, wrapping me in another hug. She finally turns and shakes Alyssa's hand.

"Nice to meet you, Alyssa. Please excuse us. We are a little territorial around here," Maggie giggles.

"Where is Logan?" I turn, asking her.

She laughs, "Megan, a hospital is no place for a baby. Logan and Rhett are at home checking on everything and hanging out until I hear something. They dropped me off here on the way, so I'll get a ride back whenever you leave. I'm not leaving you alone." She squeezes my hand.

I smile.

My family is everything.

***

A few hours have gone by and the only updates the nurses on the floor will tell us is that he is still alive. I'm half asleep with my head on Maggie's shoulder, Alyssa has walked down to the cafeteria, and Derek walked to the nurses' desk to get him another coffee when I hear wheels approaching the door of our room.

"Miss Mapleson?" An older woman in scrubs comes into view, slowly opening the door and Maggie and I both stand up quickly.

"Yes?" I question her.

As soon as the question leaves my mouth, I notice they are wheeling Collin's bed into the room at the same time. Maggie grabs my arm and we both wipe tears as we see him. He looks pale and is wearing a hospital gown with bandages all over his leg. An IV line runs into his arm, and he is hooked up to a heart monitor. Every time it beeps steadily, I feel like my body relaxes even more than just seeing him.

The staff secures his bed near the back wall while the nurse talks to us.

"He will be in and out of sleep for a while until the anesthesia wears off." She states, "He came through the surgery beautifully. Whoever was with him knew what they were doing. They saved his life with the tourniquet and fast acting CPR." She gives us a reassuring smile and leaves us alone in the room.

I walk over to my brother and rub his hair with my hands. He stirs and looks up at me. "I'm alive?" he says hoarsely with a goofy grin.

I nod and put my forehead to his. A tear falls from my cheek to his head. Maggie walks to the other side of the bed and grabs his hand.

"Don't you dare scare us like that again," she tells him sternly.

He manages to give us a small laugh. "Oh, you know me. I have to keep y'all on your feet."

We laugh at his comment. He's sounding like Collin again.

The door squeaks getting our attention and Alyssa comes walking in. She stops abruptly seeing Collin laying in the bed and wipes back a tear quickly. You can tell she wants to run to him, but she is cautious with Maggie and I here.

Maggie leans over the bed and whispers to me, "Let her see him."

I huff, but gradually pull away from my brother giving Alyssa space to step over to him.

Derek suddenly walks in from the hall and takes a seat under the television hanging on the wall and I stop when I get close to him. "Nurse says the person who was with him at the time of the attack is to thank for him being alive." I give him a slight smile. "Thank you, Derek."

He nods but is silent.

"How did you know what to do?" I ask him.

He stays silent for so long, I was about to walk away, but then sighs. "I worked as a paramedic for a few years. When you see the things I have, you learn a thing or two." He does not look at me as he takes a deep breath.

I decide not to pry and walk out to the hallway to get some coffee.

"I know you don't want to, but Alyssa needs us to be nice to her," Maggie says behind me making me jump at the surprise, fixing her a cup of coffee too at the station next to the waiting room.

I roll my eyes.

"You know if you keep doing that your eyes will get stuck that way. Not a good look for such a naturally pretty girl. I'm sure it will be hard to barrel race when you can't see where you are going," Maggie says sarcastically, with a grin.

I give her a death stare.

"I didn't even know about her," I whisper.

"And neither did I. But she is here, isn't she? She obviously cares for him." She pours some sugar into her cup.

"But they aren't engaged or married so he's our responsibility until then," I huff at her.

She stares at me blankly then takes a long exhale. "Megan, he is a grown man. He is his own responsibility. We have to let him grow up sometime and spread his wings. He would want us to be nice to her." She stares at me in that look only she can give me. If anyone else looked at me the way she does sometimes, I'd punch them.

"You are right," I whisper.

She gasps dramatically and I roll my eyes again.

"Did THE Megan Mapleson just admit someone else was right?" she laughs.

I swat at her, and we both laugh.

"Don't ever leave us again," I smirk at her.

"Deal." She winks at me as we make our way back to Collin's room.

Chapter Eleven
Megan

It's been a full week since Collin's accident and he is finally getting to go home. The doctors are really impressed with his recovery so far and he will have to come back and forth for physical therapy for the next few weeks.

After insisting to Maggie that I would be fine and her place was at home with her family, she and Logan have been tending to the farm while I have stayed behind at the hospital. Well, Alyssa and me. She will not leave his side. I have taken Maggie's advice and tried hard to be nice to her. Derek has gone back to the farm to help Logan with jobs until I get back, giving me a nice break from him grumbling. I am thankful for what he did for Collin, I am thankful for what he did for Molly, but he is still on my shit list. Something is going on with him, I just have not put my finger on it yet.

The sun is finally rising and creeping into the hospital room through the window. I decide I am going to go out into the waiting room and fix me a cup of coffee. As I walk past his bed, I notice Collin is sleeping peacefully and Alyssa stirs from the cot beside him.

She looks up at me, rubbing her eyes to wake them up fully.

"I'm just going to get some coffee," I say to her.

She nods and slowly sits up beside the bed looking back at Collin as I exit the door.

The hall is quiet, and the nurses are all at the desk giving report to the next shift coming in. It has been a long week. I have not eaten or drunk much since I have been here, and I've only sponge showered. My mind has been on taking care of Collin. I need a change of clothes, too. The ones I have on are from what Logan brought when he came and picked up Maggie when I forced her to go home to her baby. Her breasts were so swollen from not being drained. I felt so bad for her.

I smile entering the waiting room and notice it is empty, but the nurses have put on a fresh batch of coffee. They have learned it is the first thing I do as soon as I wake up.

"Um, Megan?" a hoarse voice says behind me.

I jump and turn quickly.

"Alyssa," I gasp, holding my chest, "That's a good way to get hit." I grumble turning back to put sugar in my cup.

'I'm sorry. I just wanted to talk to you for a minute," she says nervously.

I sigh. "Well, what is it?"

She rocks back and forth on her heels as if this conversation worries her. By the looks of it, she is more worried about how I will respond more than anything.

"Well, Collin is going to need some extensive therapy." She pauses, and I nod. "And he will need to be looked after all day until he can put weight on his leg again. The doctor is saying it could take up to six weeks or more," she says in a whisper.

I nod but my gut already knows where this is going.

"Well," she starts, "I live not far from here. And I want to offer letting Collin move in with me. I know you have big responsibilities at the farm and not enough help as it is." She pauses pulling nervously on a few pieces of her hair. "I want to take care of him, and he will be in great hands."

I stare at her with no emotion. Anger fuels me thinking about letting someone else care for my brother. It is my job not hers. She is not his wife or his fiancée. Until then, it is my job. I have raised him. He was always mine to look after.

Collin would want us to be nice to her.

I curse Maggie's voice in my head silently.

After a moment I look at her with a small grin. "Give me a few moments to think about it."

She nods, fixes her cup of coffee in silence, and then walks back to Collin's room.

I immediately take my cell phone out of my back pocket and call Maggie.

Ring. Ring.

"Meg, is everything okay?" Maggie says, worried, on the other end of the line.

"Hey, yes and no." I start and I hear Maggie gasp. I realize how that sounded and quickly reassure her, "No, no not like that. Collin is fine. It is Alyssa; she wants Collin to go home with her and recover with her." I roll my eyes at the thought, but Maggie does not say anything.

"Okay?" she finally says nonchalantly.

"Okay? Okay? Is that all you have to say?" I ask her. "Maggie, a stranger wants to take my brother in and care for him."

She laughs, "And I'm supposed to be upset about someone wanting to care for him?"

I can hear her grin without her saying a damn word.

She sighs, "Look Meg, I do not know the girl, but she offered. She has been there the entire time. I mean she even has his initials tattooed on her wrist. I would bet she would take care of him the same way you or I would." She pauses. "Actually, no, she would do it better because well, you know."

I gag into the phone, and she laughs.

"Give her a chance. You gave me one, remember?" She is smirking on the other end; I just know she is.

I am silent for a moment and then I huff, "I hate you."

"You love me." She laughs.

I hang up the phone and walk back to Collin's room. This conversation is going to hurt my pride a little.

Making my way through the door I hear it creak when it opens wider for me to walk through. Alyssa is sitting in a chair beside the hospital bed reading a piece of paper that we were given by Becky who came by and checked on us yesterday. It is resources for things about Collin's recovery process.

Alyssa looks up at me when I approach her, and we both look over at Collin who stirs a little in his sleep but does not wake up. Tears prick at my eyes watching him lie there. For the longest time, he was all I had. We survived losing our parents and our grandparents together. We found out we had a long-lost cousin together. He has been my biggest headache but also my biggest fan. I am not sure what I would ever do without him. But I am not the only one who loves him.

One day he will have a wife and kids that will come before me and that's exactly how life is supposed to be. I cannot protect him from everything like I did when we were kids.

Taking a deep breath, watching the girl beside him as she looks at him. She is obviously in love and cares a lot about him. She must if she put up with me all week in this hospital. I watch Alyssa wipe a tear from her eye, and she watches my brother sleep.

"You really care about him, don't you?" I ask her before I even realize the words leave my mouth.

She nods while wiping another tear, not saying a word. The look on her face is the only confirmation I need.

"Promise me I won't regret what I'm about to say," I pause, and her eyes turn hopeful. "I promise you if something happens to him, I will hunt you down and make you wish you were never born." I stare at her sternly. My body heats at the anger just by the thought.

Before I know it, Alyssa is hugging me. My arms go tense at my side, her embrace shocks me and my eyes widen.

"Thank you, Megan," she says pulling out from our hug. "I promise you I will give you updates all the time, and you are welcome to come visit anytime." She goes in to hug me again, but I stop her by putting up my hand.

"Yes, keep me updated. And I will give you Maggie's number, too. If you cannot get me, call her." I pull out my phone and get her number put in it. Once I have her contact, I send her a text with Maggie's contact info.

"I know you aren't so sure of me right now," Alyssa starts still looking at her phone saving our numbers, "but one day I hope to be a friend to you and Maggie." She smiles at me and then goes back to sit in the chair by Collin.

"What did I miss?" Collin stirs awake and we both stand at his side.

"You're going to be moving in at my place," she says to him with a grin, rubbing his hair.

And for the first time in a while, I see my brother full-on smile. A happy smile. He reaches up and pulls Alyssa in for a small kiss.

Pulling away he looks at me. "I'm shocked the warden let that fly." He smirks.

"Don't worry, I've already threatened her," I say with a wink.

Collin laughs but Alyssa does not.

Chapter Twelve
Megan

The sun is shining over Alyssa and me while we stand beside Collin in his wheelchair under the awning at the front entrance of Grace Memorial. As a miracle would have it, Collin got discharged today and as I watch Alyssa walk to her car to drive it over to us, I am trying to hide my anxiety. Allowing her to care for someone that means the world to me is going to take some getting used to.

"I love her," Collin says looking at me with a smile. He grabs my hand, and I try my hardest to fight back a tear smiling back at him. "Thank you, Meg, for letting me fly away from the nest."

I strengthen my grip in his hand and reply, "You know you always have a place to call home."

Alyssa pulls under the awning around the same time the last word leaves my mouth. A white Dodge pulls in behind her and I realize its Derek. He gets out of his truck and walks over to us.

"Maggie sent me to pick you up," he says to me, and I nod.

He shakes Collin's hand. "I'm glad you are okay, brother."

"I have you to thank for that." Collin pulls him in for a hug and Derek is shocked for a moment.

"I knew she would kill me if I let anything happen to you," Derek jokes pointing at me and everyone but me giggles.

I roll my eyes.

Derek and I help Alyssa get Collin in her car and I tell them bye one last time before they drive off.

A tear pricks at my eye watching her car pull out from the parking lot.

"He will be fine," Derek says in a clipped tone. He seems angry or even jealous. I notice neither he nor Alyssa said much to each other before she and Collin drove off but now Derek is just pure anger.

I huff. "How considerate of you."

We both walk back to his truck. I pull myself up into the passenger seat and he gets in on the driver's side.

"How has the farm been?" I ask him when we drive off toward home. "Your cousin's husband has been working my ass off," he snarls, and I smirk, thankful for Logan's extra hands while I have been gone so much lately.

"Good." I tell him. Instead of trying to make small talk with me, he turns the radio up loud enough that we cannot talk over it, and we ride home the rest of the way in silence. After the week I have had, the silence is just fine by me.

***

Home sweet home comes into view while we ride down the driveway and I get a feeling of euphoria and relaxation. Being stuck at the hospital has made me miss this place so much lately.

Getting out of the truck, I grab my bag and carry it up the porch, stopping to pet the dogs as they get up to meet me. Grabbing the door handle to the front door, I pull it open, not expecting what my eyes see before me. I look around as I make my way inside with my bag of clothes. I am shocked, stunned, and all the words above. It looks like a pigsty. The kitchen is destroyed, dirty dishes all in the sink, the kitchen table is cluttered and there's mud tracked in all throughout the house and stairs. Empty beer cans line the tables throughout the first floor.

"I'm sorry, did I forget to clean up the last time I left?" I ask Derek sarcastically; he walks inside behind me.

His hands run through his hair, "Yeah um," he starts to say nervously, "I've been so busy with work and tired when I come in, I guess I didn't take cleaning as a priority."

I stare at him shocked at what I am hearing.

Sitting my bag down beside the bottom step of the stairs, I start climbing two steps at a time until I reach the top. I am beyond speechless at the sight before me.

Footsteps are heard coming up the stairs behind me, and I ignore them while I walk into the bathroom. So many dirty towels and clothes lay on the bathroom floor that you cannot tell where the floor tile is. The shower is caked in mud and the sink is covered in toothpaste and spit.

I walk past Derek and back down the stairs quickly when Logan makes his way through the door.

"Megan! You are home!" Logan greets me and pauses looking around the place. "Holy hell, what happened here?" He looks appalled.

"Have you not been in here since I've been gone?" I ask him.

Logan shakes his head no. "Derek said he had it under control. I never thought to check." His jaw is clenched now showing me he is pissed off as much as I am over my grandparent's home being neglected.

"Did you have anything planned for Derek today?" I ask Logan.

He shakes his head no. But a grin on his face lets me know he agrees with what I am about to do.

Turning on my heels, I face Derek.

"Seeing as you have disrespected my home that I've so graciously let you reside in for the past week, alone, while I've been gone, I think it's only fair that you spend the day cleaning it." I gesture to the mess around us.

"It's not my house and I have work to do." He gestures to Logan, trying to argue with me.

I giggle angrily and Logan replies, "No. Don't drag me down with you. Megan and Maggie are your bosses over me. You'll learn quick that it's their way or no way." He nods at me with a grin and leaves us alone in the house.

"This is ridiculous. I am not a house maid," Derek says to me with a snarl.

"Listen to me and you listen good," I point my finger at him. "You do not get anything handed to you around here. You respect what you got, and you take care of it. From now on I expect you to help me keep this house clean if you're going to live in it and eat out of it," I exclaim sternly.

"Or what?" he tests me.

"Or you can leave this farm and never come back." I step back from him and gesture to the door.

"You can be a real bitch; do you know that?" he snarls at me again.

"And don't you forget it," I grin. "Now, pick which area you want to start first and get to it."

There is a moment of silence, but I don't break my eye contact. After a few seconds, Derek lets out a deep breath. "Dishes it is boss."

To my amusement, he walks over to the dishes in the sink and starts washing them. I let out a big breath myself, thankful my anger issues did not just lose me our extra help.

DEREK

I do not know why I let the house get so bad off and honestly, I blame it on my depression.

I kept telling myself, I will do it tomorrow but when tomorrow came, I put it off again.

She did not deserve walking into that after the week she had, and I fully agree with the way she spoke to me. I was out of line and needed that swift kick in my ass. But it does not mean I have to show her how I really feel. Getting her worked up is one of the things I like the most about her. Her fire is unmatched, and she is set in her ways. She is delicate and fierce all in one.

I spent the day washing all the dishes, folding laundry, and sweeping the floors. I truly know how to keep a house up—I used to be OCD about my living space, but things are different now. You do not care about things once you know how easily they can be gone. You learn to not hold things at such a high value anymore. It can be here and gone in a split second.

I watch Megan with her back turned to me. She dusts the tables, the photographs, and I was intrigued at how she carefully made sure everything was in its proper place. You can tell she genuinely loves this house, and the memories held in it.

"What are you staring at?" Megan asks me with a glare, and I realize I had been staring for too long.

"I'm not staring at you if that's what you think," I try to reassure her as I throw the rag in my hand over my shoulder.

"Looked like you were staring at my ass," she says nonchalantly as she goes back to dusting.

"Don't flatter yourself, sweetheart," I grunt at her turning back to the kitchen.

"You are nothing but a big kid. I bet you have never had responsibilities of your own. I bet you have never had to look out for anyone but your selfish ass," she exclaims to me with her hands on her hips.

I huff, "You have no idea what my story is."

"How could I?" she starts. "You are impossible to read or figure anything out about. Always this stone-cold guy who is unhappy and looks miserable. I mean, do you like guys? You seem to get along with my brother and Logan better than us women. I mean hell you even gave Alyssa the cold shoulder," she says.

"I assure you, sweetheart, pussy is all that is on my buffet." I give her a devilish grin.

She throws the towel down that she was dusting with and crosses her arms, "Are you coming on to me?" she asks me.

I laugh, "You wouldn't have to ask that if I was."

"I know all I need to know about you. Selfish, cocky, and full of himself. I bet you have never had to go through tough times." She tries to change the subject as her cheeks flush pink.

"You think you have me all figured out huh?" I chuckle.

"I wish I did," she mumbles.

In two steps I am in front of her face, "Be careful what you wish for, sweetheart." I snarl at her.

"All I wish for is for you to clean up your mess and respect this farm. You will be out of my hair after this summer anyway," she grins at me.

And before I could reply she slides to the side and steps around me, leaving me in the room by myself with my thoughts.

Damn this woman and her ability to leave me speechless.

My dick twitches.

For fuck's sake.

Megan

Derek and I spent most of the day cleaning the house, only stopping to eat a sandwich for lunch. Neither of us spoke to the other after our few harsh words earlier in the day and that is exactly how I wanted to keep it. The man infuriates me but what infuriates me the most is the way my body reacts to his anger and his voice. I do not want him knowing how I react to the alpha male act. How he could have me on my knees begging for anything by that snarl he does.

I pour myself a glass of sweet tea from the fridge and make my way out of the screen door onto the front porch, stopping to give Reba, George, and Izzy some scratches before stepping off toward the barn.

It is getting darker outside as the sun is starting to go down so I flip on the lights inside the barn so I can see better. All the horses lean their heads out of their stall windows looking at me. I walk over to my favorite girl and give her a few good scratches on the head.

"I know girl, I've missed you, too," I tell Molly.

She's getting older now and I cherish every moment I get to have with her. This year we stopped breeding her because I was afraid it was putting too much stress on her body.

I make my way farther down the barn to Crackerjack's stall and I give him scratches, too. Tiny is in the stall beside his and he nudges me for scratches as well. Tiny is Maggie's baby, but I always make sure he does not feel left out when I am out here too.

I take in the barn and the creatures around me. This is my little slice of heaven on earth and these animals fuel my soul. It is something I cannot explain to someone who does not live our lifestyle. It is just a part of who I am.

Ring. Ring.

I take my phone out of my pocket and notice it's Logan.

"Hello?" I say into my phone.

"Are you in the barn?" he asks me.

I look around confused, thinking he may be close by, "Yes? Why?"

I hear Rhett crying in the background, "I haven't fed this evening yet. Rhett wouldn't take a nap this evening and I'm letting Maggie get a nap in before she takes the night shift with him. Can you feed while you're out there?" he asks me, sounding overstimulated.

"Of course, Logan. You know to call me anytime you need my help," I tell him.

"I just know you have had a lot going on today and recently," he says, shushing Rhett.

I sigh. "We all have. But we can dodge these curve balls together, remember?" I smirk into the phone.

He laughs, agreeing with me and we both hang up quickly as Rhett's cries become hysterical.

I walk into the tack room and start filling buckets with our black feed scoop to take to all the horses. It takes a couple minutes, but I eventually get the sweet feed in all their individual buckets.

Grabbing the water hose, I walk to each stall filling up their water buckets for the night. Tiny's is the last bucket I am having to fill, and my hose gets stuck in the wood crease on the swinging stall door. Tugging on it as hard as I can, I realize it will not budge.

I grasp both hands over the hose as the water is still running wide open and pull on it with all my strength. It comes loose and all the tension I had on it drops me on my ass. The hose goes flying and before I have time to react, the water hose sprays Derek all over his face and chest. If steam could come out of his ears, I am sure it would in this moment.

"What the hell, Megan," he says to me in a growl.

I try to keep from busting out laughing. His hair and shirt are dripping water. I had no idea he was even coming out here.

My laugh stops instantly, he starts pulling his blue T-shirt off in one big swoop. The primal way that only men know how to do. Where they bunch it up from the back of their neck and pull it off from behind. My body heats up.

The water is still running, but I don't move. I freeze as my eyes are glued to all the tattoos and muscles on this man's body. I only thought he had a lot on his arms, but most of his chest is covered, and when he turns around to turn the water off, I notice his back is full of them, too.

He has an entire back piece. What looks like an angel in firefighter gear carrying a person across fire. It is colorful and some of the most detailed and beautiful work I have ever seen before with bright colors of red and orange. I stare at it while his back is turned to me.

He turns the water off at the main line. He smirks turning around and catching me staring at him. Once my eyes slowly make it to his, he gives me a devilish grin.

I gulp, still frozen in place.

He stalks to me slowly, his grin not withdrawing even just a little, and he gets so close to me that I can feel the heat from his body. Reaching around me, he grabs a towel that is laid by my head on a rack and rubs it over his face, his eyes never leaving mine.

I feel the pool of wetness in my panties. I hate myself for reacting this way about this man. He infuriates me. Why am I responding this way?

"What are you staring at Megan?" Derek asks in a deep growl.

He does not leave his stance nor his eye contact and I am afraid to move. Before I realize what is going on, he drops the towel down beside me and his thumb goes to my cheek. He runs it down to my lip and on instinct, I bite my lip timidly.

"Are you going to answer me?" he asks in a deep tone, but I am still frozen; confused to why my body is acting this way. My brain stopped working.

"I-I..." I start, "I'm sorry I got you wet." I finally say.

He leans into my ear and says, "By the looks of it, I got you just as wet." He winks at me pulling away and walks out of the barn.

I try to calm down my breathing and *what the hell* just happened thoughts.

For God's sake, I need to change my underwear.

Chapter Thirteen
Derek

How did I let my guard down? She just makes it easy. She puts me in a calm mood and allows me to feel things I never thought I would feel again.

The cold shower runs over me. After leaving the barn, it's the first place I came to. I am trying to avoid jacking off to the thoughts of my boss, standing in her barn, staring at me the way she just did. The way her mouth made an O shape made me go hard in an instant. I needed to get away from her in a hurry.

I knew exactly what she was thinking, and if I'm being honest, I was thinking the same. I wanted nothing more than to pull her over to the bales of hay stacked behind her and fuck her from behind or, better yet, have her mouth on me.

Shit.

The cold shower is not helping. I am still hard for her.

Her beautiful hair, her perfect lips, that personality of hers that keeps me on my feet, never knowing how she is going to respond to something. Her reaction shocked me tonight. I thought she hated my guts, that I was the only one who felt that way when we were around each other, but her body language told me otherwise this evening.

Taking my dick in my right hand, I start moving it over my shaft back and forth, imagining her on her knees before me with her pretty lips around me, gagging. It is not my best moment, and it will never happen again. I need this release right now. Maybe It will help me sleep tonight.

I feel my orgasm coming and the release almost makes me fall to my knees, even with the cold water pouring down over me.

This cannot happen again. I am not ready for this. It is too soon. Too much trauma persists to punish me for my past actions. The demons in my head want to swallow me up.

But Megan.

She is the calm in my storm. My anxiety is not as arrogant when she is around. Maybe it's scared of her, too.

I turn the water off and grab a towel to wrap around my waist. Stepping out of the shower, I stare at myself in the mirror. It feels like the devil himself is standing behind me, laughing.

I got you.

That's the words he's telling me, and it's the truth.

I don't deserve happiness.

I don't deserve life.

I did something I can never take back. I can never make it right. I can never ask forgiveness for because it was all my fault.

Anger builds in my stomach and tears prick my eyes.

Why could not it have been me. She was innocent. She was pure. She just loved me. She trusted me. I did this to her.

I pound the counter of the bathroom sink and my hands clench around the edges to hold me steady.

I don't deserve to move on.

The devil standing behind me is laughing harder. His claws dig in me. He knows I am his. He knows his darkness surrounds me. He knows I will never find the light.

And I don't deserve to, not after what I did.

I walk out into the hall and realize Megan hasn't come inside yet. I make it to my room and change into sweatpants. Noticing in the closet, there is an old guitar and I grab it. I have not played in years, but it used to relax me.

Pulling a t-shirt over my body, I realize I need something to drink. Heading downstairs to grab a beer out of the fridge, I open it and make my way to the back screened in porch on the back side of the house. It's been one of my favorite places to sit as the sun sets over the past week. I have not been to Hilltop since Collin's accident. It didn't feel right to be there when they have so much going on.

I start tuning the guitar and playing the first song that comes to mind, "Forever and Ever, Amen" by Randy Travis. It was always our song. Tears prick my eyes as I sing the song along with the melody my fingers play. The devil on my back felt like he was replaced with an angel and a sense of security spread over me. I knew she would hear me.

Chapter Fourteen
Megan

I let myself calm down in the barn before going into the house. Double checking all the locks on the horse's stalls and turning the lights off as I walk out, I make my way slowly back to the front porch. The stars are out and shining bright tonight, as well as the moon. I can hear the crickets chirping and a bull frog off in the distance.

My boots hit the bottom step to the front porch, Reba walks over to me and I pat her head. Her grey muzzle is showing more and more every day. I wonder if we will have her for many more years. Removing my hand from her head, she walks back over to the swing and lays down.

I make my way to the screen door, and I take a deep breath as I open the door, unsure what to do about Derek's comment in the barn. The screen door creaks when I pull it open and oddly enough, it's quiet in the house. The door shuts behind me as I make my way in, walking into the kitchen to pour me a glass of sweet tea.

Filling the glass up to the top, I put the tea jug back into the refrigerator when I notice the sound of old country music coming from the back of the house.

Walking past the living room and the staircase, I slowly get to the back door. The back porch my grandfather always sat on, but we never used after he was moved into the nursing home. It just held too many memories.

My mouth falls open noticing Derek is sitting on the back steps playing the guitar that was my grandfather's and singing. A beer sits beside him and his fingers glide across the strings of the guitar so effortlessly.

I open the door slowly, trying not to scare him but all he does is look up at me with eyes of lust. He looks emotional and I can tell something is weighing on his mind. He stops as I step out on the porch and take a seat in one of the rocking chairs.

"Don't stop on my accord," I joke with him to lighten the mood.

Derek lets out a small laugh and goes back to playing.

The critters are chirping off into the pastures and for the first time in a few weeks, I feel peaceful in my thoughts. My grandparents would be happy with how my cousins and I are taking care of this place. This farm holds dear to my heart in so many ways. How I wish they were both still here and enjoying the farm with us. My grandfather would love the way the breeding program is running, and the horses and cattle we have now. I miss their smiles and their stories. But most of all, I miss their hugs.

"Earth to Megan?" I finally hear Derek saying and I realize I've been lost in thought about old memories.

"Oh," I pause embarrassed, "I'm sorry, I was reminiscing." I give him a soft smile.

"About what?" he asks me curiously.

I am silent for a moment and then reply, "I was thinking about what it was like to grow up here. Back when my grandparents were still able to both be here." I feel a tear reach my eye and I swipe it away before it could fall.

Derek is silent for a while, he nods and plays a couple of strings on his guitar but stops and turns back to me, "You know, life is so unfair sometimes; it can change in an instant."

I stare at him. He's different tonight.

He's not an asshole.

"Yeah it definitely can be a pain in the ass," I reply, "But it can also be so beautiful. You know the same year I lost my grandparents, life reunited Maggie with us. A cousin I never knew I had. Without her here through losing the two people who raised us, I do not know where I would have ended up."

Derek sits down the guitar and stares up at me, "You would have ended up right here. Where you belong. I can see how much you love this place. The hard work you put in is unmatched."

I give him a slight grin and stand up, "I'm going to bed. Goodnight, Derek." I give him another small smile and turn heading back into the house.

Trying to shake off his words, I head into the kitchen pouring my glass out into the sink when I feel a body press into my back and hands on both sides of me on the sink. His words heated me to the core outside. For the first time since I have met him, I saw a glimpse of the real him tonight.

I jump.

"Derek," I pause catching my breath, "What are you doing?" I ask.

He bends down into my ear, and I can feel his hot breath on my neck, "Do you not feel it?" He pauses as if the words pain him, "Do you not feel the electricity between us anytime we are together? Because if you don't Megan, I swear, go ahead and kill me now because it's intoxicating. I cannot stop thinking about you."

I turn my body quickly around to where I am facing him. My cheeks are flushed at his words. I can feel the dampness in my panties from the barn but also more now.

Derek's eyes are dark with fire and my body instinctively wants to throw itself into his arms.

"Derek," I say hoarsely as my hands go to his chest, "We can't do this." I look down at his feet, afraid the look in his eyes will make me waver.

His hand goes to my chin and pulls my chin up for me to look at him, "But I want to do this."

And in that moment, my walls fall. I let his lips crash down on to mine. He is soft at first and then the kiss becomes erotic as his tongue dances around with mine. Lifting me up on the counter, his hands pull my hair back to expose my neck and his lips land on my carotid, sucking.

I wrap my legs around his waist, and he pulls back looking at me for consent and I nod, "I'm on birth control."

As if that is all the confirmation he needed, he picks me up off the counter and walks us both up the stairs to his bedroom. Sitting me down on the bed, he pulls his shirt off his body and my breathing hitches as his tattoos and tight muscles are looking at me.

I take my shirt off and stand to unbutton my jeans. Derek walks over and picks me up before I have my jeans all the way off and lays me down on the bed. I am mesmerized with how gentle he is. Taking the bottom of my jeans in his hands he pulls my jeans the rest of the way off and throws them on the floor with our shirts. I am feeling a bit self conscious because all I have on now is my black lace bra and black panties.

Derek looks down at me, taking it all in. His breathing gets heavier and his nostrils flare.

"What's the matter?" I ask him anxiously.

He leans down to me, our foreheads almost touching, and says, "I hope you know how beautiful you are."

He kisses me softly and I sit up to deepen our kiss, his hand goes behind my back and unclasps my bra strap in less than half a second.

My black lace bra frees my breasts from its captive hold and my nipples pebble. Derek takes one into his mouth and starts sucking on it, nipping with his teeth just a little to bring pain to the pleasure.

My head goes back as I moan and arch my back. Slowly, I feel his hand run down my body and into my panties. He smirks.

"I knew it." He grins at me.

"Knew what?" I ask curiously, out of breath.

"You are wet for me," he answers devilishly and within one second, he pushes one finger inside me.

I moan as his mouth crashes back down onto mine.

Sticking another finger in, he bends both fingers slightly just where he hits my g-spot, and I feel my body pool with pleasure.

Other than the few boys I dated in high school, I have never been with a man who knew what he was doing, and I would never give the cowboys in the circuit the time of day because I knew how playboy they were.

Derek has confidence seeping out of his pores and the way my body responds to each touch I'd say he knows his way around a woman.

I hear his zipper slide down and my eyes open, noticing him sliding his pants and boxers off his legs as fast as he can. My eyes widen with surprise seeing his package.

He's a big guy and I'm not just talking about his back and arm muscles.

I watch the vein that runs down his length turn erratic. He takes his right hand and strokes himself a few times while his eyes hold mine.

"I-I don't think that is going to fit." I say hoarsely, licking my lips.

Derek chuckles, "Oh, it will fit." He leans down to me, his dick rubbing over my thigh as he makes his way up to me. He kisses me softly and I can feel his cock pulse with each movement.

"I'll just have to take my time working you up to me." Derek smirks and puts his finger back inside me. Another finger and then another goes in. I feel him stretching me and each time he goes in and out he touches right where I need to be touched. My back arches and I moan as my eyes roll back in my head.

I feel my body tense up and he feels it, too. In response, he removes all his fingers and spreads my legs. Sitting himself in between my legs, he lines his head up with my entrance, rubbing it along the lips to get my arousal on it.

"You have to relax for this to work." Derek's eyes hold mine and I know he is right, so I let out a deep breath.

He slowly pushes himself in me, giving me time to adjust to his size the farther he goes.

At first, it's painful. His dick is so much bigger than his fingers.

He thrusts in and out of me until the pain quickly subsides and turns into pleasure. I lift my legs nearly to his shoulders needing him to go deeper and feel him closer. He leans down and kisses me on the lips as deep as he can.

I feel my orgasm building and as he pumps out and back in, that is all I needed to go over the edge. My muscles tighten and my whole-body tingles. I arch my back and scream out his name.

My muscles hold on to his cock as I orgasm hard, milking his ejaculation, and we cum together in a sea of soft, tender kisses.

Derek pulls out of me and gets up, making his way out to the hall and back to the bedroom. He's holding a wet washcloth, and he cleans us both up. My thoughts are all over the place seeing him so kind and passionate.

Rolling to get off the bed, he grabs my arm and pulls me back to him. "Where are you going?" Derek asks me.

I laugh, "To bed, we have to be up to do chores in the morning."

He points to the bed I'm laying on, "Seems to me you are already in bed." He winks at me.

I laugh but don't attempt to argue. I'm exhausted.

Pulling the covers up over my body Derek slides in behind me and puts his arm around me, kissing the side of my ear.

Well, there is no going back now.

***

"No! No! No!"

I'm jolted awake from my sleep by Derek screaming. He's burning up and sweat is running down his face. I can tell by the window in the room that it's still late at night by how dark the sky is.

"Derek!" I yell at him and try to shake him awake.

"No! Haley!! No!" Derek's screams sound like desperate pleas.

I shake him again to try to pull him out of his sleep and he jerks awake. Looking around in a panic, his eyes widen and I can see his carotid artery pulsing so fast in his neck.

"You're okay." I try to calm him and when my hand goes to his shoulder he jumps away from me.

"Get out!" He screams at me, and my eyes widen with fear.

"W-what?" I ask him confused.

"I said get the fuck out!" He yells again louder this time and points at the door.

I crawl out of the bed naked and try to find my shirt to pull over me.

Derek turns over on his side, away from me and pulls the covers over him. Throwing my t-shirt over my head, I run out of the room, straight to my bedroom.

Closing the door behind me, I try to calm my breathing and suddenly, I am angry. Tears fill my eyes, but I swipe them away to keep one from falling.

Crawling into my bed, I pull the covers up over my body to my chin and I lay in silence, trying to figure out what the hell just happened.

And who the fuck is Haley?

Chapter Fifteen
Megan

The sun is just rising as I get to the barn for morning feeding. I did not want to see Derek this morning, so I made sure I was out of the house before he was up. The dogs run alongside me as I make my way into the hall of the barn and all the horses hang their heads out of their stalls to greet me with neighs and kicks of impatience, waiting on their feed.

Walking over to Molly, who is standing patiently waiting on me to bring her feed; I give her a few scratches on her neck.

"Old girl, I hope you know how much I love you." I tell her and walk back into the tack room to fill up buckets of feed.

I spend the next fifteen minutes going to each stall, feeding, and watering each horse. They are all pleased with their morning breakfast.

I hear footsteps walking into the barn and I stop to see Derek entering. He looks like he didn't get a good night's sleep either after he kicked me out of the bed.

He walks up to me, and I walk past him into the tack room.

His footsteps follow behind me, and I turn quickly making my way to the tack room entrance before he walks in and traps me inside.

"Megan, I am so sorry." Derek says guiltily.

"Go start your chores, Derek." I tell him sternly.

He huffs. "Can we please talk about this?" he asks.

I look at him with rage and he steps back, "The only thing I want to talk about is what the hell were you dreaming about, and who is Haley?"

For a minute, Derek looks like he had seen a ghost, and he stays silent.

"Where did you hear that name?" he says after a moment.

I sigh, "You were screaming her name last night in your dream. It sounded like you were pleading with her not to do something." I look at him with no emotion, waiting for an answer.

But one doesn't come.

He runs his hands through his hair and looks down.

"Really? You can't just explain to me what had you so worked up last night and why you kicked me out? Because it's something to do with her," I tell him.

He's silent.

"Did you lie to me? Do you have a girlfriend, and you just cheated on her with me?" I shake my head, "For the love of God, Derek. Please tell me what is going on."

He lowers his head, "It's not what you think." He slowly looks up at me and his eyes look sad.

"Then what is it?" I ask him exhausted.

"Good morning, everyone!" Logan's cheerful voice comes into the barn, and I jump away from Derek turning to Logan.

"Have any work for Derek today?" I ask him.

He nods, "Yeah actually, I was coming to get him to help me in the pasture at my house today. Got some new fence posts I need to put up." He looks between Derek and me with curiosity, but I shake my head for him to stop it.

He grins, "Come on Derek, my truck's out here."

Derek's eyes find mine and he gives me a soft smile walking back with Logan to his truck. Once the two guys are out of sight, I lean up against Molly's stall and she lays her head over on me.

"You always know how to make me feel better girl," I say as I rub her nose.

I hear the truck ride off down the driveway, and I take a deep breath kicking off the stall and walk back into the tack room, grabbing a halter to get Crackerjack out for a ride. He needs a good workout this morning and I need to take my mind off everything.

Grabbing my phone out of my pocket, I call Maggie.

Ring. Ring.

I hear her yawn on the other end as she answers, "Megan, I don't know if you realize this, but I have a baby who keeps me up all hours of the night."

I giggle. I forget they are parents now sometimes. I don't know what it's like raising a baby.

"I'm sorry," I say grinning. "I am just looking at a very energetic Tiny who wants to get out for a trail ride with his buddy CJ."

Tiny is Maggie's horse and when he hears his name, his head pops out of his stall, ears pointing forward hoping he will be taken out of his stall, too.

And that's all she needed to wake up. "I'll be there in five," she states.

"Shit," Maggie starts again, "I can't, I have Rhett."

I frown but understandingly I am about to tell her it's okay, maybe next time when she says, "No hang on, I can put him in his pack 'n play and Logan can watch him by his truck in the shade. I need to get out and have some me time.

He is just fixing posts here by the house. He can watch him."

I smile, thankful to get some girl time.

**

The grass in the fields is swaying lightly in the wind and the saddle creaks under me as CJ's body sways with each footstep. There is not a cloud in the vibrant blue sky. A bunny runs out from under the fence post and runs back the way it came when it sees the horses. Maggie sits beside me on Tiny, who is matching CJ step for step.

After Maggie dropped Rhett off with his daddy, we decided we would take a long overdue trail ride to the back side of the pasture, letting the horses stretch their legs.

"How's mom life?" I ask my cousin as we top the hill.

She sighs, "I love my life, Megan, I do. And I am forever grateful for my blessings, but" she pauses as if she's trying to form her words carefully, "everything changes when a baby comes. Everything."

I laugh, "What do you mean?" I ask her.

Maggie looks off in front of us and then back at me, "Nothing's the same, not my body, not my routine, not my marriage. Rhett takes precedence over it all and he's a needy little thing." She lets out a small laugh.

"But you're doing amazing," I tell her, "If anyone was meant to be a mom, it's you." I smile at her.

"I just really want time with Logan alone." She laughs.

"Why don't you let me keep Rhett one night and you both go out on a date. I bet it would do you some good." I wink at her.

"Megan, I love you, but do you even know how to babysit?" She giggles, but I know she halfway means it.

"I took care of Collin, didn't I?" I cock an eyebrow at her and then nod, "Okay, bad comparison. Collin was not my fault."

We both laugh.

"Speaking of, have you heard from him and Alyssa?" Maggie asks me.

"Yes, she called me yesterday morning and gave me an update. Collin got on the phone, too, and told me to stop bothering them." I roll my eyes. "I know, I know. I'm trying to let go," I huff.

Maggie giggles.

"So, I heard from a little birdie that some tension was in the barn this morning. Do you care to explain?" She eyes me.

"I'm going to kill Logan," I snarl.

Maggie stares at me to go on with an explanation and I know she will not stop until she gets it out of me.

"You know, I'm regretting inviting you now," I growl at her.

"Shut up and just tell me," she says sternly.

We bring the horses to a stop at the top of the hill. It's the same hill Maggie and Logan were on the day they saved the calf her first day on the job. It's also the same hill Collin got hurt on. Down below you can see the whole farm and I notice Derek and Logan in the pasture working on fences. Rhett is laying in his pack 'n play. The wind is blowing slightly, and I take in the scenery around us. This is my heaven on earth. This is home. And I am so thankful for it each and every day. No matter what is going on in life, I always have home.

"We had sex last night," I say without looking at Maggie.

Maggie gasps. "You did not!"

I turn to her, and she stops looking so shocked when she sees the emotion in my eyes.

"He kicked me out of the bed early into the morning," I say calmly, but the emotion in my tone says otherwise.

Maggie looks at me confused and then back down at the men below. "Do I need to go fire him?" she asks, clearly angered now.

I go on without answering, "He was having a nightmare. He was screaming in it and sweating violently. He kept saying the word no and he called out the name Haley." I pause, "He kicked me out when I asked him about it when I woke him up and, in the barn, I asked him again and he looked so sad."

I can feel Maggie staring at me, but I don't turn to look. Her hand finds my shoulder and she sighs, "Sounds like there's more to him than he lets us see."

I nod in agreement.

I know there is, I saw it last night before the nightmare.

But I still did not deserve what he did to me.

"Well, I won't fire him yet, but I will if he does this shit again. Kicking you out of the bed? Unacceptable!" Maggie states.

I laugh and we both pull on our reins to guide the horses back down the trail to the barn and back toward the men.

Chapter Sixteen
Derek

"So, what was the tension in the barn this morning?" Logan asks me while we pull wire to the new fence post we just put in. We are over on his and Maggie's land working today. Their one-story white farmhouse in the background is in the perfect spot. They have a beautiful place by a pond. A place I could see myself in the future but knowing I do not deserve it.

"Respectfully, man, it's something I need to fix on my own," I tell Logan.

"I get it," Logan tells me. "You better not hurt her. I know she can stand on her own, but she's more fragile than she comes off. She and Maggie have been through a lot, and they are good women who care about people fiercely."

I nod but stay silent as Rhett starts crying.

Changing the subject, I ask the first thing that came to my mind. "How's life since becoming a dad?"

Logan walks over to Rhett to give him a pacifier, and he stops crying immediately. "It's the best feeling in the world, man. Having this little version of you and the person you love, it's a feeling I can't explain. I would die for either of them without a second thought. They are my entire world." He smiles at Rhett and goes back to pulling wire, oblivious to the tear that escaped from my eye.

It was all my fault.

I should not have asked that question.

"Think about having your own someday?" Logan asks and the question gut punches me. I remind myself to answer and breathe, "Uh- no. Kids are not for me."

Logan laughs, "Yeah, I thought that too. Until that test was in front of me and I saw those lines. It got real, quick. One of the scariest moments of my life, but as soon as they laid him in my arms, it was like nothing else mattered but my little family."

I can only nod.

Shut the fuck up.

Quit telling me how perfect your life is.

Mine has done nothing but swallow me up in hell.

"You okay man?" Logan asks me and I notice he's staring at me hesitantly.

"I feel sick all of the sudden. I think I'm going back to the house and see if I can cool down." I tell him walking away.

"Yeah, good idea. Maggie wouldn't be happy if Rhett got sick." He makes baby noises at his son, not giving me another thought.

My breathing slowly settles once I'm out of sight of Logan and Rhett. I sit down on a bale of hay as I reach the inside of the barn and take deep breaths.

Haley, I am so sorry.

Haley, I love you.

Haley, I miss you.

Haley, forgive me.

Those words leave my lips in a whisper as I rock back and forth on the bale of hay. My breathing getting more rigid again as I rock.

After a moment, I hear hooves enter the barn and look up to see Megan and Maggie entering with their horses. They are both laughing and in deep conversation, not noticing I'm here.

Maggie looks up as she is tying Tiny to the area the horses get unsaddled and notices me. She asks, "Are you okay?"

I nod, "Yes ma'am." I pause looking at Megan, but her eyes turn away quickly when they meet mine. I look back at Maggie, "I just got too hot out there. Needed to come in and cool down in the shade."

Megan ignores my words, taking her saddle off Crackerjack and walks it into the tack room. Maggie walks in the tack room and comes out holding a water from the fridge and hands it to me, "Here. Drink something."

I take the water bottle from her and nod, "Thank you."

She gives me a soft smile and turns from me as I twist the cap off the top and take a long sip.

Both girls ignore me the rest of the time but neither of them says much to each other; it makes me wonder how much Megan told Maggie on their ride.

I feel my heart rate speed up. My hands start to shake with anxiety.

"Why don't you go in the house where the air conditioner is on and cool down for a little bit," Maggie softly says to me.

I know she wants me to leave for Megan's sake. She still has not looked my way.

I stand and finish the last of the water. "I can do that," I tell her with a gentle nod and walk out of the barn throwing my bottle in the trash at the end of the hall. My heart beating in my chest is the only sound I hear when I exit toward the house.

The dogs are laying on the porch as I make my way up the steps and enter inside. The air conditioning hits me, allowing me to feel a wave of cool covering my sweaty body. The only thought in my head now is…

What do I do now?

Chapter Seventeen
Megan

It's been a little over a week since Maggie and I went on our trail ride. I have done my best to ignore Derek as much as possible other than times I have had to ask questions about the livestock. We both go to bed at separate times and get up at separate times. I feel like he is trying to ignore me as much as I am him.

I am sitting at the kitchen table talking to Rylee from Double J Ranch about some bloodlines we have coming up. "Yeah, I think we could do that," I tell her. "I'm still waiting to hear from the rodeo committee about nationals. But if you can send him to us, I will be happy to work with him."

"Oh great, Megan. Thank you so much. I just have too much on my hands right now with the baby on the way and not enough help as it is." She thanks me.

After she and Maggie resolved their differences, we worked with her and her husband's farm closely. They are expecting a little girl in the fall. Sometimes, if she needs help breaking colts, our stallion sires, I will take the training off her hands if she does not have the time or the room.

"If for some reason the rodeo committee calls me, Logan can take over the training," I reassure her before we part ways.

"That sounds perfect. Thanks again!" Rylee says on the other end before disconnecting.

Setting my phone on the table, I pick up my pen and start back looking through bills for the farm. I have been letting Maggie enjoy mom life as much as she will allow me and trying to do a lot of the business side myself since being home. The front door crashes open startling me in my seat.

Derek.

He looks terrified and my heart rate rises as I abruptly stand.

"Megan," Derek's voice is low and hoarse like he's trying to hold back emotion. "I need you to bring some towels and come with me, quick."

Without hesitation, I grab towels from the laundry room and run out the door behind him. I hear screams and my heart hammers in my chest as I realize who the screams are coming from.

Getting into the barn, my eyes widen, and adrenaline rushes through my veins making me shake.

Maggie is laying on the floor and blood is coming out from under her.

"What happened?" I scream, running to her.

"I don't know. She was brushing Tiny when I went out to refill waters in the pasture and when I was making my way back, she was on the ground bleeding. I heard her when I was out there and came running in from the pasture. She needs to go to the hospital. Logan was home with Rhett, but he is on his way. I need you to get over there and hold the towel under her to help stop the bleeding." He says to me and for the first time I realize he is scared. Derek is frozen in place.

"I was having issues last night and this morning going to the bathroom. It was like it was hard for me to pee." Maggie says breathlessly and her eyes look faded.

"She could have a bladder prolapse. It's common after childbirth," Derek says but still, he does not move. His wide eyes are focused on the ground at the blood.

I hear a truck fly into the yard and stop so hard at the barn gravel flies everywhere hitting the exterior walls. Rhett is crying in the back seat, but Logan runs into the barn leaving him in the truck.

"Maggie!" Logan hollers.

"Logan, she needs to be taken to the hospital," I yell at him.

He nods, "What about Rhett?" He looks around unsure what to do.

"Derek, get Rhett out of the backseat; he will stay here with us." I order Derek but he does not move. He is still shaken in place.

Knowing we cannot waste any more time, I run to the truck and take the whole car seat out with Rhett still in it.

"Go!" I order Logan as he picks Maggie up and puts her in the passenger seat of his truck.

Maggie's blood loss is making her look pale and a tear comes up in my eye when Logan runs past me to the driver's side.

"I love you," I tell Maggie as I close the passenger door with my leg.

Logan jumps in the driver seat and hands me Rhett's diaper bag, "Everything you need is in there or at the house. You know where the spare key is." he instructs me, and I nod.

"He will be fine, Logan; get her taken care of." I tell him.

Logan throws the truck in reverse and slings gravel driving out of the driveway with his truck flashers on.

Remembering I have a baby in my arms, I try to calm down my heart rate and breathing. Looking down, I smile at Rhett who has finally stopped crying. His little eyes hold onto mine.

Derek is still frozen in the barn, but I do not pay him anymore attention. Turning on my heels, I take Rhett into the house and leave Derek to take care of himself.

I take deep breaths. First my brother, now my cousin. The people who mean the most to me.

I am thankful I came home this summer.

I need Maggie to be okay...please let her be okay.

***

Maggie was right, a baby is a lot of work. I only thought horses pooped a lot. Newborns have them beat. I have laid in the floor all day with him, and he has taken naps in his pack 'n play. Thankfully, my grandmother kept all our baby things, so I had extra baby accessories here without having to go to their house.

Maggie's bladder did prolapse, and she had to have emergency surgery. Logan said he would call me soon as he could once she was awake and alert, but surgery went beautifully, and she would be able to come home tomorrow or the next day if everything continued to go well. Logan mentioned Maggie's father was getting on a plane and coming down to help with Rhett so Logan could focus on getting Maggie better once they are home.

Derek has been gone for a while on a fire call that got toned out earlier today. He did not have any work to get done here so he went to help his department.

I'm watching Rhett sleep when I hear the screen door creak, and I jump up from my seat putting my finger over my lip to tell whoever is coming in to be quiet.

Derek stands still seeing me, and he gestures to the kitchen, so we do not wake up Rhett.

I look over at Rhett who is sleeping softly in the pack 'n play and walk quietly out of the room into the kitchen with Derek.

We both stay silent for a moment and then he says, "Megan, I am sorry. Can we talk about all of this?"

I eye him curiously, but I don't say another word, prompting him to continue.

Derek sways in his stance and looks at me. "I have a lot of explaining to do, I know."

I nod, agreeing. "You do, but not right now. I am going to get a shower while Rhett is asleep." Giving him no time to reply, I walk upstairs to the bathroom and far away from him. I am angry with him today. How could he be so good with Collin when his attack happened and just freeze today with Maggie? She could have died!

I let my shower calm me down. I brush my wet hair and put it back in a soft braid. Deciding to put on my two-piece grey pajama set and make my way back down to the first floor. My heart stops when I see Derek sitting in the recliner, rocking Rhett. Derek looks like he is crying.

I slowly make my way to them trying my best not to spook Derek.

Rhett is back to sleep soundly in his arms.

Derek wipes his tears fiercely as he notices me.

I stay silent.

"You know," Derek finally says, "Today I let every bit of medical training I have go to waste." He sniffs and I listen as he continues, "I froze because Maggie reminded me so much of someone." He stops and looks down at Rhett whose lips pout for a second and then go back to relaxed.

"Haley?" I finally ask.

Derek nods. "She was my wife," he continues after a moment, "my high school sweetheart. We got married young. We always knew we wanted a life together..." he pauses again and this time I see him swallow slowly before he says the next words, "She died in a fire at our house a little over a year ago."

My heart sinks to my feet. My knees start to shake.

Oh. My. God.

Derek wipes a tear that breaks free down the side of his face. "She was home alone, and I was at the grocery store. I was sleep deprived from a call I had been on for hours and had not been home long. She was sleepy but craving some dill pickle chips, and I told her to take a nap, and I would get some after I made some tea. Unfortunately, I had left the kitchen stove eye on after making tea before I left, and it caught a napkin that I had laid down on fire. She was taking a nap in the living room." Derek wipes another tear as they flow more often now. "I came back home to fire trucks all in my yard and Captain Miller carrying my wife out of the house. She had inhaled too much smoke. She was gone." He stops trying to catch his breath and I reach for Rhett before he drops him, but he notices how shaky he is and stands to put him back in his pack 'n play. Turning and looking at me I see how blood shot his eyes are. "Megan, she was 28 weeks pregnant with our son."

Tears flow profusely down his cheek, and I have to catch him before his knees hit the floor. Helping him get in the recliner he was just in, I crouch down at his knees.

"Oh, Derek." I have tears falling now, "I am so sorry. I'm sorry for the awful things I have said to you."

He shakes his head, "No Megan, I'm sorry. I had such a fun time with you the other night. And I should have never kicked you out of the bed. You are just the first person I have been with since her and it shocked my system waking up beside you. It has always been her that I have woken up to in bed." He buries his hands into his hair holding his head.

This man is all kinds of broken.

It all makes sense now.

Chapter Eighteen
Derek

She knows. She knows and she stayed. Instead, she calmed me the best she could. She listened to me as I drained myself of tears. How could she be so good to me when I have been nothing but an ass to her?

While she was in the shower, I sat and watched Rhett sleep peacefully. I could not help but imagine what could have been for Haley and me. The life we could have had with our son. I had so many plans, so many hopes, and so many dreams. I wanted to be the best man and dad for them. That part of me is long gone, replaced by a hollow version of myself, fighting off demons every time I close my eyes.

It was all my fault.

Megan is the type of woman who deserves the world. She deserves a man who will love every part of her, and he will be able to give all of himself to her, but I do not know if I am that man.

My heart belonged to Haley. It will always belong to Haley.

She was my soulmate, the one I was supposed to grow old with.

She was the person who was the good to my bad days. The one who gave me so much hope after all the dreadful things I have seen in my career as a paramedic. But the moment we found out we were pregnant; she gave me so much more. A life away from the darkness I saw every day at work. A life I could better the world with, our son.

Instead, I had to pick out their caskets, I had to listen to people tell me they were sorry and that they would be there for me. But they still went on about their lives like everything was okay for them, while mine was consuming me whether my eyes were open or not.

Megan grabs my hand as I cry until my tear ducts are empty. And just like any great woman, she did not say a word as she walked into the kitchen and brought me back a glass of sweet tea.

Eventually, she sits across from me on the couch wiping at a tear that escaped from her eyes. "Losing people who mean the world to us is a feeling I would not wish on my worst enemy," she starts, looking at Rhett and avoiding eye contact with me. "I could not imagine what it is like losing a spouse."

I finish my glass of tea and put it on the table beside the recliner. Finally, I look at her and say, "It was my fault. The fire."

Her eyes find mine in a half second time and she gets up, walks over to me, and kneels again where she can really look into my eyes. "Don't do that to yourself," she starts. "What happened was an accident, Derek. A freak accident that you could have not seen coming. We all make mistakes."

"Yeah, but did any of your mistakes cost the life of someone you love?" I stare back at her realizing my tone was harsher than I meant it.

She takes a deep breath looks down at our feet and after a second, back at me, "No, it has not. And I am sorry if what I said was downplaying your feelings. But it was an accident, Derek. I am not sure why the universe is fucked up sometimes and terrible things happen, but I do know beautiful things come from the ashes. Life has a way of throwing us curve balls and we have two choices when it does, dodge them or let them strike us out. The choice is ours."

I turn my eyes from her and stare at the wall, "Nothing beautiful can come from losing my wife and son, Megan. I am meant to live in hell. That is my punishment for the mistakes I made."

I stand up from her taking my glass to the kitchen and putting it in the sink. "I'm going to bed," I tell her, and she nods, knowing it is best to leave me alone right now. Taking the stairs two at time, I make my way to my bedroom for the night.

Entering my room, I shut the door and make sure it is locked before walking over to my bed and laying down. My nostrils flare, and my breathing deepens. The blood in my veins is pumping through my body so fast I see stars. I want to run back downstairs, hold that woman in my arms and tell her how thankful I am to know her. How grateful I am to have met her. But I do not believe I deserve her. In another life, she could be my Haley. The one I spend my life with, the one I have children with, the one I give my heart to. My heart is damaged. It is not just bruised or a little banged up; it is nonexistent.

I buried my heart with the person I gave it to at sixteen years old and where it once sat is just a black hole. A shell of a worthless man who cannot seem to forgive himself for his mistakes because it cost him more than he could ever imagine.

Tears stream down my face and I wipe them away with my hand. Closing my eyes, my mind goes back to that day, like so many times before and replay it over in my head...

"Is that all you want from the store babe?" I ask Haley as I pour the tea, I just made on the stove into the tea pitcher for the fridge.

"Maybe some peanut M&M's too." She grins at me with that smile that will always get its way.

I just got off a thirty-six-hour shift and hardly slept since we were so busy, but my pregnant wife has cravings and it is my duty to make sure she and our son are happy and healthy.

I laugh. "You want M&M's or does he?" I question her with a smirk.

"Does it really matter?" she says back jokingly.

Touché.

I set the pot back on the stove and notice that excess water had spilled over the tea pitcher. Grabbing a paper towel from the counter, I rubbed it along the pitcher to get the water off and then set the paper towel down by the pot on the stove making a mental note to turn the stove off once I put the pitcher in the fridge.

I yawn, rubbing my hands over my eye.

After putting the pitcher in the fridge, I shut the fridge door and walk across the hall to the living room where I find Haley laying on the couch, curled up in a blanket.

"Tired again?" I ask her, bending down to kiss her lips.

"Your boy is growing and taking a lot out of me." she smiles rubbing her palm across my cheek.

"Our boy. Take you a nap babe. I will be back with all your snacks in just a few." I kiss her again before standing.

"Thank you for being the best for us, Derek. We love you so much." Haley smiles at me.

"I love you both more than you will ever know." I smile back at her.

She curls up into her blanket and closes her eyes while I grab my keys off the living room table and head out the door to my truck.

Knock. Knock.

The noise from my bedroom door pulls me out of the memory. I jump up and think twice before making my way to open it.

I can see a shadow on the other side.

Megan.

Taking a deep breath, I open the door to see her standing there, swaying back and forth, nervously.

"Derek, I..." she starts but pauses. "I want you to know that you are not alone...," she pauses again, finding her words, "and if you need to talk, I can be an ear to listen."

I nod but look down at our feet. "I don't want you to have to carry my baggage, Megan."

She puts her hands on her hips. "You shouldn't have to carry it all yourself."

I look up at her, her eyes twinkling at me. I give her a soft grin, "Thank you for caring."

She smirks, "Don't go getting a big head or anything."

I chuckle, "Will you do me a favor?"

She looks at me curiously, "Sure?"

"Can we keep this between us?" I ask her.

She grabs my hand and squeezes it slightly before letting go. "Absolutely. Goodnight, Derek."

She turns walking back down the hall and I close my door slowly until it shuts. I notice my breathing is better and my heart rate has slowed down.

She is the light in my darkness.

Chapter Nineteen
Megan

It is early the next morning and I am in the kitchen putting on a pot of coffee. Rhett is asleep in his pack 'n play and Derek is still asleep upstairs. We did not speak to each other much after he told me about Haley last night. He seemed like he wanted to be alone, and I let him after I made sure he knew he could always talk to me.

The news about Haley and who she is broke my heart. I feel like the biggest bitch for treating and talking to him the way I have lately. It all makes sense now; why he is the way he is.

He's a broken man and he thinks he does not deserve happiness again, but he does.

He has so much good in his heart; he literally helps strangers in emergencies. You cannot tell me someone who does that line of work has a black heart.

It just does not make sense.

There's more to him than he shows us.

Knock Knock.

I hear someone at the front door, and I sit down my coffee cup in a hurry to get to the door before they wake up Rhett.

"Hello, Megan," Mr. Price, Maggie's father, says as I open the front door.

I smile, "Hello, Mr. Price. Please come in. Rhett is sleeping."

"Please, call me James. We are family now, are we not?" He grins walking inside.

Maggie's father is one of the best lawyers in the state of Georgia. I always liked him more than Maggie's mom—well, adoptive mom. She is a bitch and even Maggie has nothing to do with her now that her father divorced her. After she found out she was adopted, it took some time, but she finally rekindled her and her father's relationship. He is a good man who just thought he was doing right by her.

Maggie is coming home today, and Logan called me late last night to tell me her father was flying in and would pick Rhett up and meet them at their house.

I grab Rhett's things and put them in the diaper bag as James walks over to Rhett and picks him up, smiling at his grandson.

James turns to me, "Thank you for helping my girl yesterday. I'm so glad she has you and will be okay."

I hear footsteps behind me as Derek is making his way down the stairs. He is already dressed for work in jeans and a dark t-shirt. He nods at James, but I can tell he is curious who he is.

I gesture, "Don't thank me, Mr. Price, This is the guy you should be thanking. He was out there when it happened. If he hadn't come and gotten me and called Logan, we would have never known."

I give Derek a soft smile.

James holds Rhett with one hand and puts his free hand out to Derek. "James Price. I am Maggie's father."

Derek looks shocked, but after a moment he shakes his hand. "Your daughter gave me a job when I needed one the most, sir. I have a lot of respect for her."

James nods and looks back at me. "If there's anything I've done right in this world, it's my Maggie."

"She is the best." I give him a soft grin. "If you need anything before they get home, please don't hesitate to call me."

"Thank you, Megan. I'm sure we will be fine, but Logan has already sent your number to me just in case." He thanks us both for watching Rhett and walks out to his truck heading to Logan and Maggie's place.

I stand at the kitchen door watching James drive off down the driveway. Turning to the kitchen, I notice Derek is staring at me.

"What?" I ask confused.

"You did not have to tell him it was me who came and got you," he tells me.

"Why wouldn't I? It is the truth." I eye him curiously.

He looks at me with anxious eyes. "I don't deserve the recognition, Megan. I froze up because she reminded me so much of not being able to help Haley."

I stare at him, carefully going over the words in my head knowing he's flighty right now.

"You do deserve the recognition, Derek. On this farm, we believe that nothing is random. You found Mags for a reason. I believe you have a guardian angel watching out for you." I give him a soft smile.

He shrugs. "Thank you."

I grin. "You are a good guy, Derek. You've just been through a lot. I get it. Believe me, so have I."

He nods as I turn and make my way upstairs to get ready for the day.

***

I can't find a clean pair of jeans upstairs. I basically destroyed my room looking for them. My hair is pulled up in a messy bun and I have a green tank top on. Making my way down the stairs with my cheeky pink panties showing under my tank top I hurry into the laundry room to try to find some jeans.

I sigh. I really need to do some laundry sometime soon. There are at least two baskets full in front of the dryer. I bend over to rummage through it with my ass sticking straight up in the air. Standing up, I start to put them on but feel someone behind me.

I gasp and a deep chuckle comes out of the man's mouth behind me.

"Derek!" I squeal and drop my jeans in surprise.

"Now this is a look I could get use to walking in on," he says to me, and his green eyes are dark.

In this moment, I can feel my panties becoming dampened and I sway from side to side to get it to stop. But now, the friction of my movements is making it worse. Derek raises his hand to my chin, and he rubs his thumb over my cheek. "Megan," his hoarse voice growls, "Let me make the other night up to you."

His eyes bore into mine and I gulp.

"What makes you think you get off the hook that easy?" I jokingly snarl and walk past him picking up my jeans and taking them with me trying to make it back to my room where I can shut the door and lock it.

I feel him turn and follow me.

"I want to prove to you I won't do it again," Derek says to me sternly.

I half-heartedly giggle. "What makes you think I even want a second time, not like the first was that good anyways."

Derek stops in his tracks and smirks. "Now I definitely want a redo."

He stalks to me and he gives me a devilish smile that looks like sin. The same look he gave me the night at Hilltop. My heart rate accelerates.

He leans into me just enough to where our lips don't touch and he says, "Give me a second chance."

I laugh. "What makes you think you deserve one?" I ask.

He takes a deep breath. "Because I need a chance to make this right."

All it takes is a nod from me before he picks me up and carries me to his bedroom. Each step he takes, my heart beats faster. His eyes do not leave mine but then they linger from my eyes to my lips.

"Have I told you that I have wanted you since the moment I met you when your horse trailer got hit?" He whispers to me as we enter his bedroom, and he shuts the door behind us with his foot.

I smile. "You were an asshole that day."

Derek smirks. "Only because I was trying to keep you far away from me."

I look at him curiously and he grins. "You were beautiful, Meg. I didn't trust myself to be too close to you. I like that you talked back to me and put me in my place. But I—I was not ready for anything."

He slowly drops me on the bed and glides my tank top off my body. I sit on the side of the bed in nothing but panties and my bra. Derek leans in and kisses me softly on the lips as my hands go to the bottom of his shirt and lift it up to take it off him. He pulls back from our kiss to help me remove it.

Wrapping his hand around my waist, he glides me farther on the bed where my head is near the pillows.

He comes in to kiss me and I stop him as I look around. "I'm shocked your room is cleaned and bed is made."

Derek drops his head to my shoulders, and I can feel his smile spread across his face. "Just one of the many reasons I like you. You keep me accountable to my actions. I'm sorry I let the house get messy while you were at the hospital."

"By the looks of the cleanliness of this room, I'd say you have learned your lesson," I grin.

His lips move to mine again and at once my lips kiss him back deeper than his. His tongue parts my lips and grazes over them. Stilling, intertwined in our kiss, he lowers his hand down my stomach, over my hip bone, and stops when he gets to the entrance of my panties letting his fingers linger on the fabric.

I pull back from our kiss, "What's wrong?"

His dark devilish eyes look into mine and he smiles, "Nothing. I need you to lay back and enjoy this next part."

He glides himself down my body, spreading my legs, and positioning himself in between them. I watch him as his nostrils flare and his breathing accelerates. Putting one hand on each side of my panties, he slowly slides them down my thighs and off my legs, letting them fall onto the floor. His eyes run back up my body to my eyes and he gives me an evil smile as he lowers himself down to my folds and sticks his tongue out, licking me. My back arches and I moan as my eyes roll back in my head.

"Watch me," Derek orders and it takes all my strength to obey him as the sensation of pleasure starts to pool through me.

"And what happens if I don't obey you?" I whisper down at him.

He smiles, "Megan, you are the boss everywhere else but in here I make the rules." And with that sentence he sucks on my clit. At first, he starts easy and slow, sucking and then flicking his tongue on it then back to sucking. My mouth moves to an O shape and Derek goes back to sucking. His dark, almost black, sinful eyes never leaving mine.

It doesn't take long before I feel the intense sensation of pleasure building. As he's sucking my clit, he puts a finger into my wet opening and lifts it just enough to hit my g-pot. That is all I needed to send me over the edge as my body rips out of my orgasm. My back arches and I cannot obey his order of holding his gaze as my eyes roll back and I moan his name.

He quickly gets up from me and kisses me as my orgasm is rushing through me. Coming down from the climax, he pulls away looking at me. "What did I tell you about I'm the boss in here?" he smirks.

I laugh. "Maybe I want to be punished," I whisper to him. He unbuttons his jeans, lowers them off his shaft, and within one full thrust he is in me. I let out a moan that is mixed with pain and pleasure.

Derek thrusts in and out of me faster than before and I start to acclimate to his size as he stretches me. He kisses my neck then he flips me, moving us around to where he is on bottom and I'm on top.

"If you like control so much, let me have it," he says to me and my face rushes with blood.

I quickly start riding his length slowly and watch as he cannot stop his eyes from rolling back either.

I grab his chin and grin, "Look at me."

He smiles but his eyes hold mine.

I make my pace faster and pull my feet up behind me where his cock hits in the right spot with each thrust. I feel my orgasm building again and Derek senses it, too. He takes his thumb and puts it over my already swollen clit, circling it.

My muscles tighten and our heads go back as we moan when our release escapes us at the same time. Falling over on him, I kiss his lips softly and he kisses mine in return.

"Look at you. Being a naughty girl," he jokes to me.

I laugh. "I'm a good girl. What are you talking about?"

"You are my good girl." He kisses my temple. I move off the top of him and snuggle up by his side, trying to calm my breaths.

Chapter Twenty
Megan

Derek's fire radio wakes us up from a deep sleep echoing through the house. He jumps up to grab it and my heart rate accelerates.

Dispatch: Maple EMS, Maple Fire, respond to the address of 80 Main Street, woods fire outside residence. One resident may need an ambulance after trying to put it out themselves. Other structures nearby as well.

Derek starts to pull his jeans off the recliner where they were thrown earlier.

He turns to me. "Want to go see what it's like at the fire hall?"

I jump up and smile. "Yeah!"

Grabbing my jeans and putting them on, I throw my hair in a messy bun and pull my tank top over my bra. Derek grabs his truck keys off the kitchen counter and we both run outside to his truck. He wastes no time once we are inside putting the truck in reverse and driving down the driveway toward Maple to the fire hall.

He hits the flasher on his truck as we make it out from the driveway onto the main road and he looks like a giddy little boy. The adrenaline rush is like the one I get in the alleyway on Crackerjack as he is prancing under me ready to take on the first barrel.

Pulling up to the fire hall, I see other trucks pull in and someone is pulling a fire truck out of the building with the lights on. Men are jumping out of their trucks and running to grab their turnouts. The first truck goes out and sirens blare rushing down the road.

Derek looks at me as he puts the truck in park, "Go inside and sit down. Look around if you want. We will be back soon. We shouldn't be gone long." He gives me a soft kiss and hands me his truck keys as he runs off toward the bay of the fire hall.

I wait and watch the second truck Derek is on leave out until I make my way inside. The bay is huge. It looks like five trucks fit perfectly inside with their turnouts all lining the back wall. I walk inside a door that is open in the bay and find a meeting and living area. There is a small kitchen area with a sink, microwave, and refrigerator. In the main area, there is a couch, recliner, and television. A kitchen table and chairs sit in the middle of the room.

BANG.

I jump as a loud noise gets my attention and an older man stands in the entry way of the living area. He seems confused to see me, but he knows who I am. I smile when I notice who he is. "Captain Miller." He smiles back at me.

"So, what do I owe the privilege Miss Mapleson?" He walks over to me and hugs me.

"Derek got called out to a fire. He told me I could stay here until they get back." I look at him kinda embarrassed.

He laughs. "You are good for him. He talks about you often."

My cheeks blush at his words. "I'm sorry, if I don't need to be here, I can leave." I pull Derek's keys out in my hand to show him.

"No, you are a part of our family if you're a part of his." He gestures for me to sit on one of the chairs at the kitchen table.

I take a seat, and he sits on one of the chairs across from me. He eyes me for a few moments.

I finally break our silence and say, "Did you—um, did you know Haley?"

He eyes me curiously, carefully selecting his words before answering. "I did. I'm shocked he told you about her."

I sigh. "Well, the first time I heard about her was after we slept together, and he kicked me out of the bed because he was saying her name in his sleep."

Captain Miller's eyes widen, and I blush. "Sorry, that was too much information."

He chuckles. "A little, but, yes, I knew her. Sweet girl. They were soul mates."

I don't answer, I honestly do not know if I want to know anything else.

Captain Miller gets up from his seat and walks into the kitchen. "Can I get you anything to drink?"

I shake my head no. He grabs a water from the fridge and walks back over to his seat and sits down. He opens his water and takes a hefty sip from it before continuing. "I was the one who carried her out of the house."

My eyes widen, "W-what?"

He nods. "It was a busy day. We had multiple calls that day but when this call went out, we knew it was going to be bad. We were mutual aid on their fire. Derek and Haley were not residents of Maple. They lived in Cedarville." He pauses. "Derek was not a firefighter yet. He was a paramedic with Cedarville EMS. Haley was a nurse at Grace Memorial. We worked with both of them sometimes depending on what calls we went on. Derek was off that day and had left to go to the grocery store. One of my guys had to tackle him to the ground. He wanted to run into the house for her. I packed up and took another guy in with me to find her." He takes a big gulp. "I can still hear Derek's screams when I walked out on the porch with her in my arms."

A silent tear falls down my cheek. I cannot imagine what Derek went through that day.

Miller continues, "Derek was screaming, Save her. Save the baby. But they were both gone."

He looks at me like it is the call that haunts him.

"I almost quit that day." A tear pricks his eyes. "You are the light in his darkness, Megan. Be easy with him."

I sit in silence, my brain unable to form any words after what he just said.

Captain Miller stands. "You are the only person he's brought here or talked about around us since coming here. He really cares for you." He pats my shoulder as he walks off to the men coming back.

I wipe a tear from my cheek. My heart is broken in a million different ways. For Derek, losing his wife and baby. But for Haley, for leaving this earth before being a mother. The only hope in my heart has been the thought of her and her baby being together in heaven.

Derek walks into the meeting room and sees me. I turn and chuckle as I look at his soot-covered face. His hair is full on sweat and mess. I'm sure if he did not have his turnouts on, his clothes would be dirty, too. He opens his arms to hug me, and I take a step back laughing. "No, sir. Don't you dare."

He laughs and bear hugs me before I have a chance to run away. I squirm under him, and his laugh does something to me. All the darkness his eyes has seen and all the hurt he has been through, but yet here he is laughing and smiling with me. I guess I am the light in his darkness.

***

Heading back toward the farm I notice Derek does not turn toward home; instead, he is going out of Maple all together.

"Where are we going?" I ask him curiously.

He is silent, with his white knuckles holding tightly on to the steering wheel.

"At least tell me wherever we are going, you will be able to take a bath, because you stink." I laugh and he chuckles.

"I want to take you somewhere." He does not look at me and I get nervous.

After about fifteen minutes, I notice the Cedarville sign coming into view. My head turns to Derek whose white knuckles still grip the steering wheel, but he does not look my way.

He turns his blinker on when we get close to the Cedarville Cemetery, and I can feel my heart in my throat. He is taking me to Haley.

I stay silent as the truck rides the hill up and then he stops and puts it in park. He refuses to look at me, but his hand grabs mine. "I want someone to meet you."

His hand leaves mine and he opens his truck door getting out and I get out on my side. Walking around to meet him, he grabs my hand again and he walks me over to a grave that is under a peach tree. I notice he wipes a tear from his eye.

He obviously comes here often. There is a bench by her headstone, fresh flowers in a rainbow of colors are at the head of the plot and beside it is a little toy fire truck with flowers on the back. Her headstone has an angel holding the hand of a small child around the stone with the writing and it's so beautiful it takes my breath away.

"Haley, there is someone I want you and our little boy to meet." Derek's voice breaks for a moment, and his hand squeezes mine. "I hope you know how loved and missed you are, and I know you sent Megan to me. You made sure she would put me in my place when needed and could deal with my anger issues." He smirks at me through watery eyes.

Everything around me blurs with tears. "I just want you to officially meet her," he tells me.

I turn my eyes to him in curiosity.

He smiles, "I've talked to her about you before. She knows more than I wish she did, but I feel like she already knows anyways, so why hide it?" he grins.

I smile and wipe another tear from my eye. "I promise you will never be forgotten, Haley. You or your son." I say to the grave and Derek wraps his arm around my waist.

"Thank you for being you, Megan." He says to me.

"No Derek, thank you." I kiss him softly.

And in that moment the wind picks up and a cardinal sits down on Haley's headstone. It looks at us for a moment and we feel it was her giving us her approval to go on and live our lives.

We both smile at each other and walk back to the truck heading back home to figure out this life together.

Chapter Twenty-One
Derek

Between the farm and the fire department, I have been overly exhausted and busy. Logan has had me building new pastures over by his house this past week. I have found a new respect for farmers. This lifestyle and business are not for the weak. Even though it has been demanding work, it has also been the most rewarding. Watching Megan work has been the best part of it. She puts so much love and passion into this farm. There is no doubt in my mind she was born to live here. She was born for this life.

We have not had a lot of time together lately, just us, so tonight I plan to cook dinner for her as a surprise.

I am walking through the small market on Main Street in Maple, picking out some fresh produce after stopping by the butcher's store getting some fresh meat. Megan planned to ride Crackerjack for much of the evening and my plan is to have all of this done by the time she gets back to the house. I also plan to clean the house for her, too, before she gets in.

My buggy is loaded down with fresh veggies for salad, and I grab a box of noodles from the shelf and make my way to the counter to check out. The older silver-haired lady smiles at me as she rings up my selections. "Looks like you are having a good dinner tonight," she smiles making conversation.

"Yes ma'am," I tell her and pull out my wallet.

"What are you planning for dessert?" she asks and pulls out a box from the table behind her. "We just got this handmade box of brownie mix today. It is a local's recipe. All the ingredients you need are in the box."

I was about to tell her no thank you as an idea popped into my head changing my mind. "I'll take it." I smile at her, and she happily puts it in the bag along with my produce and noodles.

"Oh lovely! You won't be disappointed." She smiles as she takes the cash from my hand.

"Keep the change." I smile back at her taking the bags as I walk out to my truck.

It is a beautiful day in downtown Maple. The street is busy with window shoppers and farming equipment passing by.

Pulling out of my parking spot, I turn my wheels toward home and let the radio play county music as my arm hangs out the window feeling the breeze. I have not felt this at peace with life in a long time. Megan has made my days brighter than I ever thought they could be. Without her in my life, I do not know where I would be, and I want to show her just how much she is starting to mean to me.

Chapter Twenty-Two
Megan

This evening, my plan is to put my focus into Crackerjack. I still have not heard back from the rodeo committee whether I have qualified for nationals or not. Honestly, it has not even been on my mind with all the things going on. CJ stands tied in the middle of the barn waiting patiently for me to saddle him. Molly's head sticks out of her stall, and it pains me every time that she is not able to compete with me anymore. I know she still has the desire and drive to.

After brushing the stall shavings off CJ, I throw on my orange saddle pad and my saddle. The girth hangs low, almost touching the ground as I walk behind CJ to the other side and pulling the girth across his underbelly and tying the saddle on; he sways knowing what is coming. After making my final loop securing the saddle, I pat his neck.

"That's the energy I like to see boy." I rub my hands through his mane.

Grabbing my bridle in the tack room, I walk over and guide it into his mouth. He never gives me any issues and takes it right as it touches him. Throwing my reins around his neck, I lead him over to the arena gate.

I've already set up the barrels for our training this evening. My plan is to do some circle work today, making sure his leg cues still respond to pressure.

Ring. Ring.

My phone starts buzzing in my pocket, and I huff, "Who could be needing me now."

Pulling the phone out, the number is out of state. I take a deep breath. "This could be them boy." I hit answer and put the phone to my ear. "Hello?"

"Yes, I am looking for Megan Mapleson?" the male voice says on the other end.

"This is she," I answer.

"Miss Mapleson, my name is Liam Cross. I am pleased to verbally congratulate you for qualifying for nationals next month. You will receive an email from us shortly, at the email you provided to your rodeo circuit, with all the information you need but we are excited to see you in Las Vegas."

"Oh, my goodness. Thank you! Thank you so much!" I try to calm my squealing to sound more professional but I'm too excited.

"You are the big talk around our community. We are all rooting for you. Have a blessed day, Miss Mapleson. We look forward to meeting you," Liam says.

I thank him again and we both hang up the phone.

I pat CJ's neck, "This is all because of you boy. I knew you were special since the moment you were born. We are going to do big things."

Crackerjack bobs his head in agreement.

Grabbing my reins and saddle horn, I put one foot in my stirrup and swing my other leg over to the other side. CJ immediately starts to prance under me.

"There's my cocky boy." I smile at the muscle memory of his prance as I guide him into the arena, ready to get some work done.

***

I'm giddy as I make my way back to the house after CJ and I spent a few hours working on some training. It is almost dusky dark now and I notice I have not seen Derek for most of the evening. Stepping up on the front porch, the dogs wag their tails and pick their heads up from their laying positions. I pet each of them as I make my way to the screen door. Stopping in my tracks, I notice through the screen door that Derek is in the kitchen cooking. He is a full tatted alpha male in his boxer shorts, shirtless, and with his cap turned around backwards as he is standing at the stove cooking something that smells heavenly.

The door shuts behind me and he turns slightly to look at me grinning. "About time you came inside," he smiles at me.

I laugh. "Do you seriously have to look that hot while cooking?"

He smirks. "Thanks for the confidence boost." He turns the stove off and walks over to me giving me a soft kiss on the forehead.

"What are you cooking?" I ask him curiously.

Derek stays silent. Instead, he turns around with a bowl of noodles and spaghetti sauce in another. A fresh cut up salad is already sitting on the kitchen table. He sits the bowls down at the table and takes the seat next to me.

"Oh, this looks delicious!" I yell out of excitement.

He laughs, "Also cooked dessert but you'll have to wait for it until you eat."

His look is stern, and I wonder to myself if I want to tease the bear or let it go. My intrusive thoughts win, and I ask flirtatiously, "What if I want dessert now?"

He eyes me, his eyes growing darker by the minute and then he stands up grabbing a bowl off the bar. Walking back over to the table he stands in front of me. "Trust me?" he asks, and I nod my head.

"Use your words, Meg."

"I trust you," I tell him hoarsely.

Derek crouches down in between my legs and sits the bowl down on the floor at my feet. My breathing hitches when I notice it is a bowl full of chocolate brownie mix.

He sticks his finger in the bowl and pulls it out placing his fingers near my lips. "Suck it," he demands, and my eyes widen.

I bend forward, pulling my tongue out to lick a little bit of chocolate off his finger. Then I put the whole finger in my mouth, sucking it gently. Derek's eyes widen while his adam's apple rises and falls. He looks like he is about to pounce on me.

Instead, he puts his finger back into the bowl. "Take your pants off," he demands and I almost protest but instead I do as I am told, intrigued at what is about to happen. I stand and unbutton them while gently pulling down the zipper. Slowly letting them glide down over my butt and fall down my thighs. Once my pants are off, I sit back down, opening my legs. He starts tracing his chocolate-covered finger up my right inner thigh toward my center.

His eyes never leave mine as he lowers his face toward my right thigh and trails his tongue up to my center, stopping right before my panties. I can feel my core heating and my panties already feeling drenched.

Doing the same thing again on the other thigh, I think I may pass out if he keeps up this teasing me.

His tongue gets so close to my center again. He pauses and runs his tongue over my panties at my clit and my hips buck. He pulls away and goes to stand, "Well, let's eat dinner."

My eyes are starring daggers at him, and he laughs.

"I'm not hungry anymore," I say with a pout, and he sits the bowl of chocolate down, walking back over to me.

"What do you want cowgirl?" he asks jokingly.

I laugh and stand, putting my hands on his chest and turning us around so his back is to the chair I was just sitting in. I push on him to sit, and he thankfully does not try to stop me as he grins.

"Good boy," I smirk, and he chuckles.

Taking my finger and slowly sticking it in the bowl of chocolate, my eyes never leaving his, I lick my lips and bend down spreading his legs as I position myself in between them.

His nostrils flare watching me kneel in front of him.

I smile at his boxers. "Those need to be gone."

Derek takes a deep breath and slides his boxers down over his hips. His length springs out and my heart races seeing he is hard for me.

I do this to him.

Running my chocolate-covered finger down his length and making my way back up to the tip, I run it around the head. Taking my finger and putting it in my mouth, I suck on it getting the excess chocolate off.

Derek's nostrils flare even more.

Our eyes stay locked as I lower myself down to him and kiss the tip of his cock. It jerks in appreciation. Slowly opening my mouth in an O, I gently guide the tip into my mouth while licking the chocolate off.

Derek's head goes back, and a deep purr leaves his lips.

I cup his balls with one hand, and I massage them back and forth as his length disappears in my mouth.

"Oh, God," Derek whispers and I giggle.

My giggle hums in my mouth and he jumps up from his seat taking himself out of my mouth fully.

He pulls me up to him and kisses me.

"Megan, I swear, if you don't take your fucking underwear off right now and sit on my cock I'm going to bust," he growls in my ear.

I follow him back to his seat and he sits back down, bringing me to him as he kisses me, and I straddle him.

Sitting down slowly, letting him stretch and fill me, I pull away from our kiss and let out a hoarse moan.

He lets me do all the work as he circles his thumb around my clit. Grabbing a handful of my hair, Derek pulls my head back, so he has access to my neck. My eyes roll back as he sucks on my neck and his length fills me fully.

I can feel my muscles around him tighten as my release comes and I let out a loud moan but his sucking my neck and circling my clit does not stop.

"That a girl. Cum for me. Milk me," he whispers into my ear.

I feel him twitch inside me as my orgasm milks his and we cum together in the kitchen while the food is getting cold on the table.

"Now I can eat," I smirk at him coming around from my release and he pushes my hair out of my face.

"Round two then?" He jokes and I swat at him slowly removing myself from his lap.

I slap him in the chest playfully.

"Seriously though, I need to call the old lady who works at the market and thank her for the brownie mix. She was right, I was not disappointed."

I bust out laughing.

Chapter Twenty-Three
Megan

After our feast at the dinner table, we watched a movie on the couch and right before bed we made love again.

Love.

That's what it feels like. We have not said the words yet, but I can feel my feelings growing for this man. We are in bed after he cleaned us up after sex and I'm lying on Derek's chest running my hands through his chest hair.

"Oh!" I say excitedly, "I forgot to tell you since your kitchen shenanigans distracted me earlier. I got the phone call earlier from the rodeo circuit. I'm going to nationals!"

I look at him with a smile of excitement, but I can't tell what he is thinking. His face is emotionless.

"What's wrong?" I ask him concerned.

But Derek remains quiet.

I sit up and search his eyes but the emotion I saw just less than ten minutes ago is gone.

After a moment of silence he asks, "When do you have to go?"

I'm not sure where this is going but I answer, "In a few weeks."

He slides out from under me and sits up on the side of the bed and throws his t-shirt on but no words leave his lips.

After a moment, He nods. "For how long?"

I'm still puzzled as to why he is asking this. "Well, depends on a few factors…," I start but he moves away from me.

"Derek?" I ask him with worry.

"I guess this was bound to happen," he says, and I still don't know what he is talking about.

"What do you mean?" I ask.

"We were just fuck buddies anyways, right? You'll be gone and won't be back for awhile. I was just your little plaything until you could get back out there on the road?"

I'm shocked at the words he's saying. "What are you talking about?"

"Just go, Megan," he says sternly.

"No, not until you talk to me," I tell him.

"I said get out." He looks at me with a hateful stare.

"I swear to God, Derek. If you throw me out of this bed again, I will never be back in it. Make your choice, now." I fight tears back from my eyes.

He is silent for a few seconds and without turning to me he points to the door, "Get the hell out of my room, Megan."

I slowly get out of bed, put my t-shirt and pants on, and walk out of the bedroom. Before going out the door I stand with my back toward him and whisper just loud enough for him to hear, "You know, we all have a shitty past. We all have things we wish we could change. We all have something broken within us. But it's what we do with that brokenness that matters."

I slowly make my way down the hall to my room. Once I'm inside, I close the door and lock it. My body slides down the door and tears unleash from my eyes.

I guess he does not love me.

***

Ring. Ring.

I can feel drool on my pillow where I cried myself to sleep last night. The ringing of my phone breaks me free from my sleep and I sit up looking for it anxiously. Tossing back the covers, I find it just in time to answer before it stops ringing.

"Hello?" I answer half asleep and fully heartbroken.

"Megan? What's wrong?" Collins voice on the other end makes me tear up.

"Oh nothing," I answer wiping a tear away from my eye. "How are you doing? Recovery going well?" I ask my brother trying to take the questions off me.

"Actually, Alyssa and I are getting out of the house for a little while today. Other than going to therapy and to get food, we don't get out much and doctor says I am improving well. I'm going stir crazy and the doctor said it would be good for me to walk around some. We are going to come by the farm and see everyone if you all will be home."

I smile. I miss my brother.

"Yes! Let me call Maggie and we can all have supper together tonight. It will be good for us all." I smile at the thought of my whole family together again.

"Yes, sounds great!" Collin excitement radiates through the other end. "Alyssa is asking if she needs to bring anything," he asks me.

"Just tell her to take care of you and I'll take care of the rest," I laugh.

Collin and I hang up the phone and I hurry to dial Maggie's number.

Ring. Ring.

"Megan, this better be an emergency. Rhett is still asleep." I hear Maggie's hoarse voice answer on the other end.

I giggle, "Oops, sorry. I'm just so excited. Alyssa and Collin are coming over to spend the day and eat tonight."

I can hear the sheets rattle on the other end. It sounds like Maggie is getting out of bed, "Logan! Get up! Collin is coming over!"

Logan huffs as he stirs awake on the other side of the phone and happiness overwhelms me at how close we all are. Just the thought of my brother coming home makes us all happy.

"This will be the best day!" Maggie squeals from the other end and we quickly get off the phone.

I jump up out of bed and run out into the hallway smacking right into a large person.

"What the hell, Megan?" Derek asks me, half asleep.

"I should be asking you the same thing," I bark. "My house, my bathroom," I sternly state as I hurry inside and slam the door shut.

"Fine, I'll piss off the back porch," I hear Derek snarl from the hallway.

Ignoring him, I quickly turn the shower on and take my clothes off. I need a bath after last night. I need to wash him off me and start this day fresh.

***

"Knock knock" I hear a female voice coming through the front door as I start down the stairs.

I smile seeing my brother and Alyssa coming through the front door. He is on crunches but he's here and that is all that matters to me.

I run up and hug him almost knocking him backwards. "Collin, I have missed you so much!"

He chuckles and points to Alyssa when we pull out of our hug. "This one has been taking good care of me, Meg. I think you would be pleased."

Before I realize what I'm doing, I throw my arms around Alyssa's neck, and she is just as surprised as I am.

"Thank you for taking care of my baby brother," I whisper to her.

She nods unable to make words.

"Make yourself at home," I tell them. "I need to go warm up Crackerjack this morning." I smile at my brother. "I qualified for nationals."

He grins at me and says, "I knew you would!!"

"Y'all go, show Alyssa around the farm. I bet Maggie and Logan would love to see you, too." I gesture to the door trying to get them out of the house before Dereks grumpy mood makes Collin question me. "Make yourself at home. We will all eat supper here tonight at the main house." I smile to Alyssa as I pull my boots on and walk out the door.

Opening the front door and walking out on the porch, I look around to see if I see Derek. My brother is home, and I do not want anyone to know about last night. I'll deal with it later. For now, I want to enjoy this time with my animals and my family.

The dogs all follow me off the porch and toward the barn. Molly's head sticks out as she greets me good morning. Once I enter the barn, the other horses follow suit and start nickering.

"I have fed them already." Derek says to me walking out of the tack room jumping on the Ranger.

"Okay," I reply walking by him and into the tack room.

Grabbing a halter and a brush from the pile we keep them in next to the saddles, I see Derek walk back into the tack room grabbing keys for the Ranger.

"I won't be here for supper tonight," he says to me sternly.

My jaw clinches and all I can muster out of my mouth is, "Good."

He grabs his keys and storms back out of the tack room, turns on the Ranger, and rides off into the pastures to do his work for the day.

Crackerjack is staring at me as I walk out of the tack area and over to him. I rub his nose. "You are the only guy I can trust, boy."

I kiss his nose and he bobs his head making me laugh.

***

I watch from the arena as Collin and Alyssa drive off in his truck through the pastures heading to Maggie and Logan's house. He must really love that girl if he is letting her dive that truck. Throwing his hands out the window he waves at me and whistles. I laugh at his goofy butt and wave back at them. Alyssa must have all the patience in the world to put up with him.

It's almost lunchtime when Crackerjack and I get done with our training and I finish it by giving him a good soak down and bath. Collin and Alyssa went all over the farm today in his truck and they finally made their way back to the barn as I was finishing CJ's bath.

"That is a beautiful horse," Alyssa says as they enter my sight.

"Thank you," I smile. "He is a brat sometimes."

Collin chuckles, "He is a brat all the time and you spoil him to where he thinks it's okay to act the way he does."

Crackerjack pins his ears at Collin; Alyssa and I both laugh.

"He takes care of me, Collin. He deserves the pampering," I state.

Alyssa walks around the barn and pets all the horses. Tiny sticks his head out of the stall, and I look up just in time to see him nuzzle her.

"You want to ride him?" I hear Maggie's voice come into the barn.

She is slowly moving but recovering well from surgery like I knew she would. Logan comes into view behind her with Rhett in his arms.

Alyssa looks frightened, "Oh, no. It's okay."

Maggie gives her a sincere grin and walks over to her and Tiny.

"He is the best boy. Took care of me when I first arrived here. I promise he will take care of you." She rubs Tiny's nose, and he lays his head over on her.

Alyssa looks at Collin and he says, "You were just saying the other day how you wished you had horses growing up."

She rolls her eyes at his statement. "Okay. Let's do it."

I make sure Crackerjack is not too wet as I put him back in his stall to dry and take his halter off. Closing the gate to his stall I walk over to Tiny and put the halter over him to bring him out to the saddling area.

Alyssa suddenly looks so fearful.

We never tie our horses completely when we saddle them. A few loops around the iron bars on the stall walls is all we do in case they get spooked. We do not want them breaking their necks trying to sit back on their hind end to get away from something.

After brushing Tiny and throwing the saddle pad over him I hear the Ranger coming close.

"Logan, will you go flag Derek down and tell him a horse is out here. To park it outside the barn until we are done," I ask him.

Logan, with Rhett still in his arms, walks out to meet Derek. Logan starts yelling and cussing in rage and the next thing I see is Derek running the Ranger straight into the barn and Tiny sits, completely loosening the halter rope, and takes off through the barn, out the other end.

Thankfully, he stops at the end where grass starts and I grab him, walking him back into the barn.

Logan comes running inside and hands a crying Rhett over to Maggie.

"What the fuck dude!!" Logan screams at Derek who looks confused.

"What?" Derek asks.

"I was trying to get you to stop because we had a horse out in the hall of the barn." Logan walks up to him closely and points his finger at Rhett and Maggie. "You better be happy neither one of them are hurt. So help me God, I would end you."

"I just thought you was coming to give me some shit about what I did to Megan last night." Derek says sternly getting off the Ranger and walking the key in the tack room.

Logan grabs his arm and Collin walks over with his crunches, they both give him death stares. "What the fuck did you do to Megan?" they all, including Alyssa and Maggie, say in unison.

I roll my eyes, but Derek's eyes widen and go to me.

Jerk. He thought I was going to out him.

Maggie turns to me, and I just shake my head for her to stop.

Logan steps toward Derek. "I won't ask you again."

Derek's adam's apple rises and falls, and he shakes his arm loose from Logan. "I don't have to tell you shit. You still have your wife and son. You don't have any idea what hell I've been through. I'm out of here." Derek walks away from us and into the tack room. I hear him throw the keys down and he storms off out of the barn and jumps in his truck. The gravel flies as he tears down the driveway leaving only a trail of dust behind him.

Alyssa looks at Logan with tears in her eyes, "Just let him go. This is how he deals with his emotions. He leaves. He has been through a lot."

Now I'm wondering what she knows that she is not telling me.

Chapter Twenty-Four
Derek

I do not know where I'm driving but I needed to get far away from Magnolia farm. The past few days with Megan had been the best days I've had in a while. I was starting to see myself here with her long-term. My feelings were growing deeper every day.

I loved waking up to her sleepy self every morning; I loved cooking dinner with her every night. She was showing me so much about life that I was missing. I was starting to feel whole again without feeling anxious about it.

But when she said she was leaving? My mind spiraled out of control. I had let my guard down with her. I knew nothing lasted and nothing stayed the same. That it was not worth putting time and effort into things when you never know when they will be taken away.

She was leaving.

My heart hammers in my chest.

I grab the steering wheel as I drive my truck down Main Street wondering where to go. I notice Captain Miller's truck is at the fire department, so I decide to pull in.

He is sitting in the kitchen alone when I walk into the lounge, and I debate if I want to step inside or not. Taking a deep breath, I knock on the door announcing my entrance.

"Hey buddy, wh-" Captain Miller starts, but notices my body language. "Derek? What's wrong?" he asks.

I walk over to the refrigerator and grab a water out while staying silent. Jumping up on the kitchen counter to sit, I open my water and take a sip before responding. "I really thought I was going to be happy again."

Captain Miller just looks at me to elaborate.

I huff. "I was starting to really care for Megan. Life was going so well. Then last night, she gave me news that she was leaving because she qualified for nationals."

Captain Millers eyes perked up, "That is amazing! Her grandfather would be so proud for her right now!"

I eye him sternly. "It is not great."

"And why is that?" he asks curiously.

"Because she's leaving me. Like all things, everything I love leaves me." I look stunned after saying it.

And for the first time, I realize how I really feel about her.

"Well, it's about time you realize you love the girl." Captain Miller chuckles.

"I can't love her. My heart isn't worthy of love anymore." I shake my head in disagreement.

Captain Miler laughs. "Boy you do not get a say-so over what your heart feels. What did you do when she told you about nationals?" he asks me, knowing I have done something stupid.

"I kicked her out of bed," I say, embarrassed.

He shakes his head in disapproval. "When are you going to learn that it is not all about you, Derek? Yes, something tragic happened to you and no one is trying to look over that, because it was horrific. But you cannot live your life stuck in the past. Haley would not want you to. If I learned anything about Haley it is that she was all about living life to the fullest. She would want you to do the same. Be thankful for the time you had with her, look back on the good memories, but also make new ones, too. Death is coming to all of us; no one gets out of here alive. What we do with the time we have is what matters. Life's too short to live in the past and not tell those we love that we love them." He pauses. "You are not the only one who went through something tragic. We see tragedy all the time with the line of work we do. But sometimes, beautiful things are made from the ashes when you allow it."

I grin. "Megan said the same thing awhile back."

Captain Miller chuckles. "She has been through a lot, too, Derek. Life has not always been easy for her and Collin, but they made due with the cards they were dealt. She's a good girl with a bright future. I'm sure she would want someone in her corner when all her dreams come true."

"I would love to be in her corner," I mumble.

He gets up from his seat and pats me on the shoulder as he walks to the kitchen. "Boy, you fucked up this time. I'll be shocked if she lets you back in the house." He laughs and my heart goes to my feet.

"I got scared," I admitted.

"Of course you did," he says, grabbing a drink from the fridge. "But love is scary. You are giving your heart to someone and trusting them to protect it." He pauses. "But you know what is scarier? Not listening to those feelings. Not telling those you love that you love them. Not living the life you are given. Because one day, you will wish you did, and it will be too late. Regret, son. That is the scariest thing."

"No, the scariest thing is losing the person who your whole world revolves around." I stand and walk out without another word.

Chapter Twenty-Five
Megan

Today has been good for my soul. After Derek left dramatically, we took Tiny out into the arena and let Alyssa ride a horse for the first time in her life. The way Collin looked at her really emphasized his love for her. My little brother has turned into a man in a blink of an eye and Alyssa really seems like the right person for him.

Logan, Collin, and Maggie won't stop scolding me about Derek. I have not told them what happened, and they cannot stand not knowing. Thankfully, they have not pushed too hard on the matter knowing I will cuss them all if I feel like I am being pressured.

I'm setting the dinner table as everyone sits on the front porch and talks. Maggie and Alyssa have been major help today in the kitchen and Collin has spent some time with Rhett and Logan.

"Can I help you?" Alyssa's voice comes in from the front door as it closes behind her slowly.

I shake my head no, but I refuse to look up at her.

She sighs, "Megan, he is not a bad guy. He has just been given a rough deck of cards is all."

I look up at her with tears in my eyes. "How do you know Derek?"

She takes a deep breath, and her eyes turn glassy with tears. "I'm assuming since he's been so upset lately, he's told you about Haley?" she asks me, and I feel like someone just took the breath out of my lungs.

All I can do is nod.

She shakes her head with understanding and sighs again. "Haley meant a lot to both of us."

She pauses and wipes a tear that escaped her eyes. "She was my twin sister."

My eyes widen and I slowly place the plates in my hand on the table and walk over to Alyssa who now has tears streaming down her face.

"Oh, Alyssa." I put my hands on her shoulders looking into her eyes as tears leave mine. "I am so sorry."

It all makes sense now, the way he was acting around Alyssa at the hospital.

She wipes another tear. "I know how much Maggie and Collin mean to you. Haley meant that to me, too. She was my person. My best friend. It was always her and me against the world. It was devastating losing her and my nephew I never got to meet."

I pull her into a hug, and she hugs me back.

Pulling out of our hug she searches my eyes. "But the amount of hurt we feel from losing a sibling, parent, or grandparent… its nothing compared to losing a spouse we give our heart and life to." She pauses searching my eyes to make sure I understand. "Derek and Haley were soul mates. They dated all throughout high school. Derek told me when they were seniors he was going to marry her. She would be the mother of his children."

Tears fall down mine and her face.

"I'm not excusing his behavior by any means," she states, "because, Lord knows, he has a temper. But he's lost. I could always go home and hang out with friends and my parents to get away from the grief. He went home to an empty bed, Megan. He went home to memories of her. He lost everything he thought his future was going to be. I could not imagine coming home and not having Collin there after being with him so much these weeks. I'm sure Maggie could not imagine the same about Logan. I'm Haley's sister and losing her was hard enough; I cannot imagine how he feels being her husband." She pauses and continues, "Losing their home, too, was even worse. All those memories just vanished with her. The pictures, the memorabilia, the little souvenirs from vacations, all gone. One mistake cost him everything and it haunts him with every breath he takes."

I look down at the floor and back up at her. "He took me to meet her. He took me to Haley's grave."

She looked shocked and then smiled. "He must really care for you then. For the longest time he wouldn't allow anyone but himself to go out and visit her gravesite. He went down a dark road, Megan. My father and he got in a huge fight. It was hell for us for a while. Sounds like he found a light in you, and something scared him off."

She searches my eyes.

"I told him I qualified for Nationals, and he blew up in my face. He kicked me out of bed," I tell her.

She shakes her head, "Sounds like something he would do. He is afraid of people he cares about leaving him again. It's a survival mode he's put himself in. As far as I know, you are the only person he has been with since Haley."

I straighten up and walk back over to the table and pick the plates back up. "Well, that's the second time he's kicked me out of the bed, and I'll be damned if it happens again."

She chuckles. "Make him grovel for it, Meg. Don't let him come back easily."

I smile up at her. "Thank you for being good to my brother. I'm sorry I was so mean the first time we met."

She chuckles before opening the screen door to the porch. "Oh girl, don't be sorry. I would be worried if you didn't give me a tough time."

***

Everyone is around my dinner table together. Laughter escapes the lips of those I love around me and my heart could burst into a million pieces. Rhett is asleep in the pack 'n play in the living room.

"Collin!! You did not!" Alyssa says to him, laughing.

"Look, it wasn't like that. I had no idea she was in the shower. I had to shit!" He looks so embarrassed as we tell Alyssa stories about when Maggie came to live with us.

Logan and Maggie chuckle.

"Y'all stop embarrassing me in front of my girl!" he tells them.

"Nah man, you let me get beer poured on me the first time I met Mags, you deserve this." Logan laughs.

"If I remember correctly, Collin did warn your ass," I tell Logan jokingly.

"Oh my gosh. Not sweet Maggie!" Alyssa laughs.

"Sweet my ass," Logan says and Maggie hits him over the top of the head.

Laughter is just what we needed today.

"Think we need to fire Derek," Logan says changing the subject after a minute.

I look at him in shock and so does Maggie.

"Logan, it's okay. We aren't going to do that," I tell him.

"He clearly did something you don't want to tell us about." He looks at me sternly.

Maggie puts her hand on his shoulder to calm him down and says, "Logan, I understand you're concerned. We all are. But she is a big girl and can handle herself."

"Well, I agree with Logan," Collin chimes in.

We are all silent for a while.

"I know I'm just an outsider here," Alyssa starts to say and we all turn to her, "But if I may, Derek has been through a lot more than he lets on. He lashes out when he is afraid of his emotions." She pauses, "I know Derek because he was married to my sister. He lost her and their home to a house fire he caused by accident. She was 28 weeks pregnant." She eyes us and everyone else is stunned at her words. "He has been through a lot. We all have. I'm not excusing him, but I do know he comes with a lot of baggage." She picks up her drink to take a sip.

Maggie wipes a tear from her eyes turning to Logan, "That's what he meant by you still have me and our son. Logan, I couldn't image if we were in his shoes."

"He better not try that shit again," Logan says hoarsely, and he stands, kissing his wife on the top of the head and walking into the living room, picking up Rhett, holding him close. Maggie follows him.

"Why have you never told me he was married to Haley?" Collin asks Alyssa.

She shrugs. "Not my story to tell. I'm only going to bat for him now for my sister's sake. I promised her at her funeral that I would go to bat for him. She would want someone fighting for him."

Collin pulls her in for a kiss.

I know the person I need to talk to.

***

After dinner, I let the girls clean up the kitchen and I hit the road in my truck. The moon is bright tonight and more full than normal. The sky is so clear and only a few stars are in the sky.

I make my way down Main Street, noticing Derek's truck is at Hilltop. I sigh at the thought of what he is doing but I keep going out of Maple city limits.

After fifteen minutes, I'm pulling up the driveway to my destination. I cannot even believe I am doing this. Looking out at my surroundings, I turn my truck off and open the driver's door.

The wind is blowing just enough to give a cool breeze, and the only light is the one from the post on the driveway and moon. I take a seat on the bench, taking a deep breath before I say, "Hey Haley. I hope it's okay that I am here." I pause trying to find my words. "I—um, I care a lot about Derek. But this is not where I beg you to send him back to me. I believe you already did that. He is just too stubborn to allow it to happen." I stay silent for a moment. "Okay, I know I'm rambling, but it's just because I love him. I want to live this life with him. I was going to ask him to go on the rodeo road with me before he did what he did." I huff. "Please remind him he is not alone. Please remind him there are people who care about him. Please remind him that it's okay to continue loving and missing you while loving me." A tear slides down my cheek and I wipe it away. "I think that's what he is most afraid of. Loving me and forgetting you. I won't let him do that. You and y'all's son will always be a part of our life." I'm silent again and an owl hooting in the woods startles me. "Your sister is an angel. She is dating my brother Collin, which I'm sure you already knew, but she is someone I feel like I could be good friends with someday." I sigh. "I honestly feel like you and I could have been really good friends, too. Take care of our guy. He needs someone looking over him. I wish I had met you before now. Even if it meant he had you back. I would want that for him more than anything."

The wind picks up and my hair blows in the breeze. I smile. "Thanks, Haley."

I wipe my tears and stand up, I turn and look at the small grave beside Haley and smile, "Watch over your daddy little guy. He misses and loves you so much."

Giving one last look at the graves, I turn and walk to my truck. Opening the door, I grab the flowers I picked from our flower bed near our porch and lay them on each grave. Then I turn and get in my truck to head back home.

Chapter Twenty-Six
Derek

The aroma of cigars and country music plays in the background as I sit alone wallowing in my emotions sitting at a table near the dance floor.

I am a mess.

After talking with Captain Miller, I could not bring myself to go back to Magnolia Farm, so instead I turned into Hilltop and decided drinking away my pain is what I need.

People pass me in a blur as my focus stays on my glass beer bottle in front of me…well the now-embarrassing hoard of empty beer bottles that cover the table before me.

"Jesus, man. Bad night?" Cade, one of my brothers in the fire department, says as he approaches my table, beer in one hand and a brunette in the other.

"Yeah, something like that," I grumble, as I down the little bit of beer left in the bottle in my hand.

"Man, if you need a ride home, I can get a ride for you. Might be best if you finish up that beer so you can sober up," Cade says to me.

I huff, "I don't need a babysitter, man. Thanks though. Go have fun."

Cade moves away from the brunette in his arms and leans into me. "Don't be stupid tonight, Derek. Too many people care about you."

He stands and grabs the brunette, walking off from my table.

I laugh to myself; no one cares about me.

As the blur of people continues to pass me by, I watch the couples interact with each over, laugh with each other, and some even dance. They do not even realize how easy all those emotions can be taken away. In a split second that happiness can be turned to anger leaving you in survival mode with every breath and every move.

It's what we do with the ashes, Derek.

Megan's words flood my mind. How am I supposed to move on from what happened to Haley? How am I supposed to be happy again? I want to, Lord knows I do…but I do not deserve it.

It was an accident, Derek.

Megan's words come flooding in again.

My heart rate picks up, my hands start to shake.

I've got to get out of here.

I stand, leaving the beers where they sit and make my way out of the bar, ignoring everyone who tries to grab me or stop me as I make my way to my truck. Climbing inside, I shut the door and lock it.

Putting it in reverse, there's only one place I'm going right now—to talk to her.

***

The crisp night air is chilling on my arms as I jump out of my truck and close the door. I open the door behind the driver's side to the back seat and grab a blanket and pillows. I used to do this often but have not in a while.

For so long, the bed was a lonely place. The nightmares were too rough and when I would wake, alone, it was even harder. Her snoring was the most annoying thing, but when it was gone— I couldn't sleep. Her crazy nighttime routine, plugging her phone in multiple times because it had to hit a certain number, was annoying but when it was not there anymore, I missed it. Life was no longer the same and when you have been with someone for most of your life, it shocks your system to the core to have to find a new normal.

I thought I was finding that in Megan. My new normal. But the moment she mentioned leaving, losing her scared me. My heart was finally opening to someone else, for the first time since Haley, and it was scary to think of it being broken again.

Walking up to Haley's headstone, something catches my eyes; fresh flowers laying near her headstone and our son's.

I know those flowers.

I've seen them every day for weeks.

I've watered them.

I've watched them grow.

She came to see Haley.

Tears break loose and I fall to my knees.

What have I done?

I crawl up near the bench that sits in-between the two grave plots and I lay there for the rest of the night, in the middle of my dead wife and son, crying. Shedding away the emotions for the life I once thought I had and the life I most likely just threw away.

Captain Miller was right; regret is the scariest thing.

Chapter Twenty-Seven
Megan

When I got back home from the graveside, Derek was still gone. Alyssa and Collin stayed for a little while after I returned, and Maggie and Logan took Rhett home before I got back. It was nice hanging out with my brother and his girlfriend for a little while and he informed me he was going to be moving in with her permanently.

At first, I was not okay with it, but once I thought about what Alyssa told me before dinner, I knew it needed to happen.

I'm standing at the barn as the sun comes up the next morning wondering where Derek is. His truck is still gone, and he never called to tell me he wasn't coming to work today. Im starting to worry about him. The sky is a beautiful shade of yellow and orange as the sun peeks over the mountain and I watch for a moment as it rises.

I turn, hearing a truck coming up the driveway and notice it's Derek. He parks by the house and gets out slowly, wearing sunglasses. I know he sees me, but he instead ignores my presence and walks toward the front porch.

"Where on Gods green earth have you been?" I ask him with my hands on my hips standing outside the barn.

He huffs, "None of your business."

Jesus. He looks hungover.

His clothes are all dirty and he honestly looks like he slept on the ground last night.

"You better get you a cup of coffee from the kitchen and come outside ready to work. We have things to do today." I yell at him.

He waves me off and goes inside the house.

I give him about ten minutes, and he never returns outside. By now, smoke should be coming out of my ears from how pissed off I am.

I walk up to the house quickly and step inside. He is nowhere to be seen. Climbing the stairs two at a time, I notice he's lying in his bed when I reach the upstairs hallway.

"You've got to be fucking kidding me," I say to him pushing the door open wide with a thud.

"Leave me alone, Megan," he mumbles to me.

"No, sir. You don't get to talk to me that way in my home." I toss the covers off him. "We all have sad stories, Derek. We all have things we wish we could forget. My parents died. Did you know that? No, you don't because you've never once asked. Do I miss them? Yes. Do I let it keep me from running this farm and continuing what they built for me and my brother? No. You have let yourself get so swallowed up in your own self-pity that you have not even thought about the people around you. Everyone has something they are grieving, Derek. Get your ass up and get to work or get the hell off my land," I yell at him.

He sits up in anger. "You wouldn't dare," he threatens me.

"Try me." My nose is almost touching his.

He stares at me for a moment, and I step back giving him room to decide.

He scowls at me. "Fine. I'll be out at the barn."

I cross my arms as he walks past me and out of the room.

Holy hell. He wants to stay.

***

I've managed to ignore Derek all day long. He has worked on fences in the back pasture and put some new boards up around the yearlings' stalls. Crackerjack and I have been able to get a good training session in today and I'm starting to prep things for nationals.

"Hey, Megan!" Rylee's voice comes through the barn as I walk out of the tack room.

"Hey! I was not expecting you 'til later this evening!" I say, hugging her, "and look at you all glowing."

She smiles. "I'm so ready for her to be here by now, I'm miserable."

Her husband, Cane, walks in with the gorgeous colt we are going to be breaking for them the rest of the summer. He is going to be tall like our stallion, his father.

"Which stall you want me to put him in?" Cane asks me.

"The one beside Crackerjack is fine." I point to the stall, and he nods, walking the colt over to it.

"You will have your hands full with him," Rylee laughs. "Hope this is not any trouble."

"Nonsense," I start. "We will be just fine. You just take care of you and that little one."

She smiles grabbing my hand, "So thankful for y'all at Magnolia Farm."

I smile back.

"Come on babe," Cane says. "Let's go see Maggie, Logan, and Rhett before we head back home."

He helps lead his wife back to the truck and they both thank me again.

I walk back into the barn and put some feed and water in the stall for the new colt and continue cleaning and packing for nationals.

***

It's been a few hours since Rylee and Cane left Maggie and Logan's. I saw their truck and trailer head out a while ago. Finally ready to go sit down myself and get me something to drink, I head back toward the house. Reaching the front porch, I'm startled as a tone goes off in the house and I run in to see what is going on, quickly realizing its Derek's fire radio.

I hear the dispatch say there is a grass fire down the road, close to our property line.

Oh, no. My cattle.

I quickly grab my phone and call Derek, but he does not answer.

I try again.

No answer.

WTF. I could need help.

So, I call Logan.

"Hello?" Logans voice is on the other line.

"Hey! Do you see Derek out there anywhere? His radio is going off and it's saying a grass fire by our property line. I'm worried our cattle are going to get hurt."

"Yes, he is up here by the house. I'll go let him know," Logan says.

"Tell him when I call him, he needs to answer." I roll my eyes as I mumble the words.

Logan huffs, "Yeah, I'll be sure he learns his lesson."

And with that, the line goes dead.

A few moments later, I hear the four-wheeler drive up to our barn and Derek's truck tears off to the fire hall. I can see the fire out there now. It is dangerously close to our pastures.

Ring. Ring.

"Megan, Logan is coming down to the barn. He is going to grab one of the horses and see if he can herd the cattle back to the house. Will you go with him? I don't like him going alone and I can't leave Rhett." She sounds worried.

"Yes, I'll head there now."

I meet Logan at the barn and we both saddle up our horses and make our way as fast as we can to the pasture near the fire. The fire truck and lights spook the horses a little, but we are able to stir them where they need to go.

A mama calf and her baby are close to the pasture line where the flames are, and I take lead going to them.

A firefighter in full gear and a hose, walks close to the pasture fence as I get close to the cattle and says, "Megan, get your ass back to the house. It's not safe out here."

I'm startled, then I realize it's Derek.

"You are not my boss," I yell back at him.

"Get the cattle back and stay the fuck at home," he yells at me, and I huff.

Who does he think he is telling me what to do? He's not my husband or my boyfriend.

Logan and I are able to steer the cattle back to the house with ease and load them into the corral until the fire is out.

"What was all that about?" Logan asks me, gesturing back to where Derek is.

I sigh. "You know, between kicking me out of the bed and then trying to dictate my every move, I really think he needs some bipolar meds." I roll my eyes, but Logan just stares at me.

"HE DID WHAT?" Logan looks pissed.

I wave him off, "It's old news."

"No. That fucker doesn't get away with that." He scowls.

"Really, Logan; it's okay. He has a lot going on," I say calmly.

"I don't care what the fuck he has going on, Megan. A real man should never do that." He looks out to where Derek is.

"Logan, how would you feel if you were in his shoes?" I ask him.

He drops his head. "I guess I would be in a pretty dark place." His voice cracks. "I don't even want to think about it. Maggie and Rhett are my entire world."

I smile. "And they are waiting for you at home. I can finish here. Thanks for the help!"

He smiles and heads back home after telling me bye.

I know Derek has a lot going on in his mind, but in an instant, I regret taking up for him. Logan is right; he should not be able to get a pass for his actions just because he is hurt. He is hurting people in the process, and I am not sure I can keep taking up for him.

***

It's a little after lunch before we are able to let the cattle back out in the pasture, but the fire department does a wonderful job getting the fire out quickly and no other structures were hurt.

I'm sitting at the kitchen table when the screen door opens a few hours after I notice the fire trucks went home. I've eaten a sandwich for supper and got a shower, so I am ready for bed.

I look up from my phone and see Derek standing there with soot all over his face and I giggle.

"Not funny." He gives me a small grin.

"It kinda is." I giggle again.

He walks over to the table and sits down. "I'm sorry for being an ass." He stares at me.

I look up at him but don't say a word.

"I don't have any excuse for my behavior. It was wrong of me," he says, and I still sit silently.

After a moment I say, "You know, if you would have given me time to explain the other night, I would have told you that I was going to ask you to come on the road with me."

He stares at me with a sad expression.

"You ruined that opportunity," I state and get up walking upstairs to my room to leave him to fend for himself for supper.

I have never in my life felt more empowered than I did in that moment but right now more than anything I wish my mother were here to talk to or my grandmother. I need their advice.

Shutting my bedroom door behind me, I climb into bed and pull the covers over me to my chin. My brother is moving on with his life, my cousin has her own family, and I'm alone. I want a love like my grandparents had. I must be tough for so many people; for once I want someone to be tough for me. Someone who will take care of me when things get tough and not run away. The only constant male I have in my life is Crackerjack. I giggle at that thought of my goofy boy. He may knock over barrels during our runs but at least he's never broken my heart.

I hear footsteps walking up the stairs and the shower turn on in the bathroom. My body heats up knowing he's in there naked and how I would love to just forgive him and get in the shower with him. But I can't. I cannot let myself let him get an effortless way out when he acts the way he does. He will learn that his actions have consequences.

Chapter Twenty-Eight
Megan

I wake to the smell of biscuits, gravy, eggs, and sausage cooking downstairs. The memories of waking up to my grandmother's cooking takes over and a tear peeks through my lashes as I wipe it away.

I miss her and my grandfather every day. This house reminds me so much of them and one day I hope I can bring the next generation to grow up in it. I could picture mine, Maggie, and

Collin's children running and playing in the yard. Having the best summer swimming in the pond over by Maggie and Logan's house like we all did, riding their horses through the mountainside, and sitting down together for family meals. First, I need to find a man that will be willing to go that extra mile with me some day.

Smiling at the thought of someday, my stomach feels a little nauseous and I look around looking for a water or something to drink but there's nothing on my nightstand.

I slowly get up and put a sweatshirt over my tank top, making my way downstairs to see who is cooking up a storm in my kitchen.

Stopping dead in my tracks, I see Derek standing by the sink in grey sweatpants, a black tank, and an apron. I giggle. This is a new look from him. He turns as he sees me, and he smiles, "Good morning."

"Did you do this?" I gesture to the table that holds a bowl of gravy, a plate full of eggs and sausage, and a baking sheet full of homemade biscuits.

He grins. "I did. Hope you like it."

I take a seat at the table as he pours me a glass of orange juice and sets it by my plate.

"It smells lovely." I take a sip of the orange juice and start to fix my plate. I am starving and the nausea has subsided, thankfully.

Derek fixes his glass of orange juice and sits down at the chair across from me. He waits until I am done with my plate and then starts putting food on his.

We sit and eat in silence. I am starving and don't even take the time for him to finish fixing his plate before I dive into mine. The food is heavenly. If I hadn't seen him in the kitchen, I would have thought an older Southern woman cooked it. Someone like my grandmother.

We finish eating and Derek takes my plate and his to the sink.

"It was delicious," I state. "Where did you learn to cook like that?" I ask him.

He looks at me like he is unsure if he should respond and then says, "Haley and Alyssa's mama. My parents were not very present in my life. My father chose drugs over me and my mother left us when I was young. Haley and her family were all I knew." His eyes search mine before he continues. "Her father was the only dad figure in my life. I was so mean to them when she died. I shut them all out when I should have helped them heal, too."

Derek drops his head.

I grab his hand.

"Don't you dare do that to yourself. You were grieving, Derek. You went through something so unimaginable, and I do not think any of them hold it against you. You lost your wife and your son at the same time. You shouldn't have to apologize for the way you grieved something like that." My eyes search his.

Derek's eyes look up at me and I see them sparkle with a tear stuck, ready to fall out. "When I met you, something snapped in me. I wanted to be close to you, get to know you. I just felt like I was cheating on my heart. Megan, I am so sorry for what I did to you." His thumb comes up to my chin and rubs my cheek. "I love you. This has been hell not knowing how you feel about all of this. And me."

My hand grabs his wrist as his thumb glides over my cheek. "I love you, too, Derek. I hope you know how much you mean to me. But I'm not ready to let you in. You hurt me and you never gave me a chance to explain anything before kicking me out of the bed." I take a deep breath.

"If you had a daughter and she came up to you and said, Daddy this guy I like had sex with me but then threw me out of his bed after hearing something he didn't like from me, without letting me explain, how would you respond?" I ask him, my eyes search his.

He drops his head again and his thumb stops moving along my cheek, "No questions asked. I would beat his ass and smile in my mug shot." He pauses, then continues, "And I would tell her that a real man would not even think of hurting her. He would know how sacred it is for someone to give their heart to you and be vulnerable with you; you should always respect them for it. I would tell her that the right man would never make her question her worth."

I smile. "Then how do you expect me to just forgive you that easily over something like that?"

His hand drops to his side and he steps back, "You shouldn't forgive me, Megan. You should go and live your life. You should find a man who will always listen to you and make you a priority. But I want to be that man for you. I want to grow in all the ways you need me to. Because you are the light in my darkness, and I am lost without you."

I take a deep breath and let his words sink in before saying, "I know. Derek, but right now, you are my darkness. You are not even aware of how your actions are affecting me. We are not okay right now and I don't know if we will ever be. You need to give me space."

He nods in agreement and starts picking up plates from breakfast. "I understand and agree. Don't worry, Meg, I will give you time."

I leave him to clean up his mess and go back upstairs to my room to get ready for the day. Feeling like a big weight just came off my chest but also disappointed that I didn't take the easy way out. I cannot and I will not. A relationship is made up of forgiving and sacrifices but there is a limit to them, and I will not tolerate the way he has been treating me.

I want a man who will protect me no matter what. Put me first no matter what. Be able to help me run a home without me having to worry about him throwing me out when I do something he does not like. He needs to grow the fuck up and realize life sucks but it's the things we have now and the people we have now that keep us going.

Chapter Twenty-Nine
Megan

It's been a week since Collin and Alyssa came by to see us all. CJ and I have been working every day to get ready for nationals and I am so tired. I feel like I don't get enough sleep between chores, training, and all the responsibilities around here.

It's about lunch and I am walking back from the barn to the house. Derek meets me on the porch with a sweet tea and I thank him as I approach and take it from him. We have been pleasant with each other, and he's been trying like hell to get me to not be mad at him anymore. It is not that I'm mad; I am just disappointed.

He stares at me as I take a sip and I can tell he wants to tell me something, but I just keep sipping my tea. The dogs are running around the house chasing one another and I can see one of the horses in the pasture rolling in the grass.

"Oh, I got you something." Derek says going into the house and quickly returning with a bouquet of flowers. I smile at him, and he hands them to me already in a vase.

"Well, thank you." I grin and walk in the house and set them on the table.

"It's congratulations on making nationals. I'm sorry I never said that when you told me. I wish I could take my words back." His eyes search mine.

"I know. I'm just not ready to talk about this." I tell him and he nods.

I pick up a candle that is sitting on the table, light it, and sit it down next to my flowers.

"They are beautiful Derek, thank you." I smile at him and take my empty tea glass to the sink.

He stands in silence for a moment and then walks to the door. "I'm going to town to get our monthly feed pick up since Logan and Maggie are out on a family shopping day with Rhett. Do you need anything while I'm gone?" he asks me.

"Actually, pick me up some lunch if you don't mind. I don't feel like cooking. I'm so tired lately," I tell him and he nods.

"Anything in particular you want?" he asks me and I shake my head no.

"Surprise me," I laugh. And he smiles, walking out the door.

I hear the door close behind me and I take off my boots setting them by the front door. I yawn and grab some Tylenol out of the cabinet. I feel like I'm getting a headache.

I walk up the stairs two at a time and go lay down to take a nap while Derek is gone to see if this headache will go away. I just have not been feeling right the last few days.

***

DEREK

I smile walking out of Nana's with Megan's lunch. The feed has been picked up and am now about to head back home to my girl. At least, I hope she will be. I care deeply for her. I love her. But my heart feels so selfish when I think of Haley. I know she would want me to be happy, but my heart and head are at war. Even if I have to spend the rest of my life trying to get back in Megan's good graces, I will. She deserves that from me. I have fucked up big time and I hope someday I can show her I can change and be what she needs me to be.

Reaching my truck, I hear sirens as my fire department runs a truck down the road.

Ring. Ring.

My phone startles me and my heart rate accelerate as I read the name that comes up.

"Captain Morgan? Everything okay?" I ask him. He knew I wouldn't be around this week. I had too much to do at the farm.

"Derek, it's Magnolia Farm. House fire. Is anyone inside?" My heart sinks and I rev up the engine getting on the road.

"Megan was when I left." My voice is a whisper.

I grab my fire radio from the passenger seat and turn it on in time to hear the dispatcher say, "Caller is advising structure fully evolved."

My knuckles are white as I grip the steering wheel, Megan's food from Nana's flying all over the seat.

No. God. No. Don't you dare do this to me again.

I do not remember the drive down the driveway and I do not remember parking my truck. All I remember is jumping out to the sight of the farmhouse I was just standing and talking to Megan in fully engulfed in flames.

A truck pulls up slinging dirt, and Logan and Maggie get out. Maggie is holding Rhett, and she is hollering at me, "Where is Megan? She's not answering her phone."

Fear takes over my lungs, "She was inside when I left."

"Oh, dear God, NOO!!" Maggie screams and Logan and I tear off toward the house.

Captain Morgan jumps on Logan and Logan tries to fight him off.

"I can't have you doing something stupid and getting yourself hurt," he tells Logan and me while Maggie is screaming and crying.

"Logan what about me and Rhett!! You cannot do something stupid like that." Tears flood her face. As Logan and Captain Morgan focus on her and the other fireman are busy bringing hoses out, I take off inside the house.

"Derek! Don't be stupid!" I hear Captain Morgan's voice on the outside as I enter.

"I'm not going through this again," I yell back coughing.

I look around as the fire has engulfed the living room and kitchen, but the stairs seem to be okay for the moment, just smoke everywhere.

I pray she is in her bedroom with the door shut.

Please God, let the door be shut.

Taking the stairs as fast as I can, I pray they do not give out from under me. I make it to the top and smoke has risen all the way up. Getting on my hands and knees I crawl to her room and reach up to open the door and crawl in fast. With it being closed it trapped everything on the outside from getting in so far. I slam the door shut again and see her lying in bed. I rush over to her side of the bed.

Picking her up, she does not wake up and I feel her pulse.

Thump, thump.

I let out a breath; she is alive.

"Baby, wake up." I tell her touching her face. She just lays limp in my arms.

"Stay alive, Megan. I need you to stay alive. I cannot live without you," I say as I grab a blanket from her bed and throw it around us.

I tighten my arms around her body and take a deep breath as I get ready to open the door again. If I want to make it out alive, I need to focus on getting back down the stairs.

I grab the door handle and as the door opens wide, smoke starts rolling in from the ceiling and I duck as much as I can with her in my arms, sprinting down the stairs. My coughing gets worse as I make it to the bottom of the steps and my vision is going darker the closer to the outside we get.

It takes everything in me to get through the front door out to the front of the porch. Megan and I land on the ground by the porch steps with a thud.

"Oh my God, Megan!" Maggie screams.

The house starts to fall in around us and we jump back. Smoke spreads everywhere; it's all gone.

"The house!!" Maggie yells as tears pour down her face and Logan embraces her.

"Here give her this." One of the medics says giving me an oxygen mask to give Megan to see if she will come to.

I start coughing again. "Might need to take you some deep inhales of it, too," the medic says sternly at me.

I nod, agreeing.

But my priority is Megan.

It will always be Megan.

This is my second chance. A do-over. A new life. I almost lost her. Just like I lost Haley. How could I be so stupid and selfish?

I had a wonderful life with Haley, and she will never be forgotten, but I'm allowed to be happy again, too. I almost lost it. As God as my witness, I will never come that close again even if I have to get on my knees and beg for her forgiveness.

Megan starts to come around and I grab her face and kiss her.

"Derek? What happened?" she asked me hoarsely.

Maggie comes into view and Megan looks confused. "I never thought I'd hear your voice again." Maggie's voice breaks and tears leak around her eyes. "The house is gone, Megan. But you're alive and that's all that matters."

Megans eyes widen, and she looks around, "No. How did that happen? I just went and took a nap." She holds her head. "Oh god, I lit that candle."

I hold her and say, "It's not your fault. It was an accident. You are okay and that's all that matters."

"It's not your fault either, Derek." Megan mumbles to me and tears fill my eyes. She's referring to what she told me the night I told her about Haley. She's making sure I see the irony in this.

But it's neither of our faults.

Tears fill her eyes, and she starts to cry.

EMS comes over to us and asks us if she wants to be checked out at the hospital.

I nod and she looks at me in protest. "No ma'am. You don't get a say so. You were not feeling good before this happened anyway. You need to be seen by someone."

Maggie nods agreeing. "Listen to him, Megan. Let them check you out."

Megan stays silent as the medic puts her on a cart in the back of the ambulance and hooks her up to monitors and then she says, "Where am I going to live now?"

"She acts like she doesn't own all this land." Collins voice says from around the side of the ambulance smiling at his sister.

Maggie hugs him and Alyssa appears, too. "I'm glad you're okay," he tells Megan, and she smiles, reaching her hand out to him.

I notice he grabs it and squeezes it tight.

He lays a hand on my shoulder and mouths, "Thank you." And I nod.

"Anyone riding with us?" The medic asks and I jump in the back with my girl.

Chapter Thirty
Megan

I wake up to the sound of beeps. Slowly opening my eyes, I look around the room and try to get my eyes to focus. It's blurry at first but I quickly realize I am in a hospital room and laying on a hospital bed.

Beep beep.

I look up at the monitor beeping above me. It's my heartbeat and my IV pump.

"Hey…" A familiar voice and face come into view, and I smile.

"Derek, w-wh…" My voice is hoarse, and I cough.

"Hang on, let me get you some water," he tells me, reaching for his water next to where he has been sleeping. By the looks of it, we have been here a few days. He's made a bed on a small cot.

He brings the bottle of water to my lips and slowly lifts it so I can drink some of it.

"Oh good, she's awake." Another familiar voice comes from the door, and she walks over to my bedside checking my fluids.

"Becky?" I ask and she grins. "You gave us quite a scare, Meg." She grabs my hand and squeezes it. "They got you to the hospital and your blood work was out of whack and you were severely dehydrated. You passed out in the ER and have been in and out for a while, sleeping." She pauses. "All of you Mapleson kiddos need to chill with making this a regular visit."

I chuckle and she look at Derek. "Have you told her?"

He shakes his head no and I look at them back and forth. "Tell me what?"

Becky pats my hand and looks at Derek. "I'll give you two some privacy. Call me when you are done, and we will get her some food to try to eat."

She gives me one last smile and walks to the door shutting it on her way out. I turn to Derek whose eyes glisten at me. He takes my hand in his and smiles while rubbing his thumb over the top of my hand.

"What I'm about to tell you," he pauses, "I need you to stay calm okay?"

My eyes widen and I can feel my heartrate spike. The beeps pick up on the monitor, "Are Maggie and Collin okay? The horses? What's wrong?"

Derek brushes the hair that just fell from my eyes, and he takes a deep breath. "Everyone is fine, Megan. I need you to focus on calming your heartrate and taking care of yourself. It is not just you anymore."

I scan his face with confusion and his eyes glisten with tears. "Megan, you are pregnant. The doctor estimates about five weeks."

My eyes widen and I think I might throw up. The tiredness, the headaches; they all make sense now. I knew I could not be tired just from farm work. I have done this work my whole life. I knew something was slowing me down for a reason.

"I-I'm…pr-pregnant?" I grab my stomach and tears fill my eyes.

Derek grabs my hand and tears leave his eyes. "No one else knows. Other than Becky; she got the report and told me. I wanted to tell you before we told the family."

"But I'm on the pill." Then my mouth widens in horror. "I can't remember when the last time was I took my pill. I have been so anxious about nationals." I look at him. "You're the father, in case you doubted that part." I chuckle and he laughs.

"Well, God, I had hoped so." He laughs and kisses my forehead. "I'm happy about it. I was hoping you would be, too. I am so sorry about your grandparents' house. I know there were many treasures in it that you wanted. But I am so thankful you and the baby are okay." He pauses as a tear falls down his cheek, "Megan, I am so sorry. I am sorry for everything. All the shit I did to you. I almost lost you. I almost lost you and our baby." His tears are falling heavy now. This broody, alpha, tattoo-covered man is falling to pieces at my bedside. It is like I can physically see how broken his heart is outside of his body. He grabs my hand. "For as long as I live, you will come first. You and our child. This is my second chance at a life. A life with you. A chance to be happy. I want to make you happy."

Tears slide down my face and I grab his hand. Not able to form my thoughts into words, all I can say is, "Me, too. Thank you for coming in after me."

"You are the light in my darkness, Meg. I would walk through the deepest trenches in hell if it meant getting to you." Derek picks my hand up and kisses it.

"Come here and kiss my lips." I pull Derek up to me and he kisses me deeply. I don't want to pull out of our kiss for air; he is my air. My breath of fresh air. He is just as much the light in my darkness as I am his. I pull back from our kiss, both of my hands on his cheeks, and look him in the eyes, "We both get a second chance. Let us do it right this time."

***

"Welcome to the mom club!" Maggie screams on the other end of our FaceTime. Derek and I are lying in the hospital bed together while we FaceTime Maggie and Logan to tell them the news. They have been taking care of things at home while Derek is here with me. I was informed that he was keeping them up to date on everything and Maggie was annoying him with texts every hour for updates, too.

"Knock knock." Alyssa's voice comes from the door and Collin walks in behind her, without his crutches.

"Hey!" I say and turn back to my phone. "Collin and Alyssa are here, Mags. Give Rhett our love. And we love y'all! Hopefully, they will discharge me soon."

"Collin, she has a surprise to tel-," Maggie's voice screams on the end and I cut the phone off as quickly as I can while Derek is laughing hoarsely.

"What was that?" Collin asks, confused, and I gesture for them to take a seat in the chairs by the bed.

"Everything okay?" Alyssa asks, concerned, and Derek and I smile at each other.

"How do you guys feel about being an aunt and uncle?" I ask them as I twirl the bottom of my hair and Collin looks at Alyssa wide-eyed.

"Depends," Alyssa starts and Collin nods to her. "Depends on how you guys feel about being aunt and uncle, that is if y'all are together again or not." She laughs and I roll my eyes.

"W-wait." My eyes widen and I look at Derek who is giving me the same look. "You're not pregnant are you?" I ask gesturing to her, and she nods with tears in her eyes.

"Are you?" She asks and all I can do is nod as tears stream down my face.

"How far along are you?" I ask her and Collin replies, "Doctor says about seven weeks."

"We are five," Derek says excitedly, and he and Collin jump up hugging each other. Alyssa runs over to me and hugs me tight. When we pull back, we are both crying.

"Some groveling he did." She smirks at me, and I chuckle in laughter wiping tears from my eyes.

Derek hugs Alyssa tight and she cries even more. "She's good for you, Derek. Haley would be happy knowing you have Megan."

Tears spring again in his eyes, and he rubs her shoulder, "Thanks, Alyssa. Kind of crazy we could be in-laws again someday."

"Okay, okay. Enough making me cry or I'm going to be dehydrated again. We've got to FaceTime Maggie or she will kill us for keeping all of this from her," I say picking up my phone.

"Actually, we are heading there after we leave here to tell them," Collin says, and I smile at the thought of them wanting to tell us the exciting news.

We all sit and chat for a little while when suddenly the thought dawns on me. "Oh shit. What about nationals?" I look at Derek concerned. I have to be there in less than two weeks. I cannot back out now. Not with all the work I have put in.

Derek puts his hand on my knee and says, "We can ask the doctor before we leave. We will not let you miss it if we can help it."

***

Shortly after Collin and Alyssa left, Becky came in with my discharge papers. An OBGYN doctor came in to give me an ultrasound to see if we could hear the baby's heartbeat. They were not confident we would hear it as they do not like doing tests before six weeks at least, but sure enough, the sound was music to our ears. Derek leans over me with tears streaming down his face.

The doctor informed me that since I was already riding horses before I knew I was even pregnant that I could continue doing what I was doing, just needed to be careful lifting heaving things and eat more while taking my prenatal vitamins.

I'm sitting in the passenger seat of the truck as we turn down the driveway to the farm and Derek looks at me, "Now understand, it is gone. Brace yourself for what you are about to see." He tells me and tears fill my eyes as the once beautiful white farmhouse comes into view all on the ground. The house my grandparents raised us in.

Tears flood down my face, and Derek grabs my hand.

"Was anything saved?" I ask him but his silence is all I needed to confirm nothing at all was left.

All those pictures, letters, clothing and so many memories. I notice Maggie, Logan, Collin, and Alyssa are all standing around waiting on us to come into view and Derek pulls up beside Logan's truck. Collin and Logan walk around to the passenger side and open the door to help me get out.

"Feeling, okay?" Logan asks me and all I can do is nod.

"I can't believe my stupid self lit that candle and took a nap with it lit under those flowers." I say through the tears and Maggie puts her arm around me. "What matters is you and sweet little peanut are okay," she says patting my tummy.

She hugs me and Collin comes over, putting his arm around both of us. We stand there for a moment, in front of our grandparent's old home and the memories flood through my mind.

The years of me and Collin playing on the farm, riding the horses through the yard, when Maggie first arrived when I brought her that morning, Logan and Collin beating the shit out of her ex-fiancé in the front yard, the ambulance pulling off with my grandmother and my brother.

Us Mapleson kids have been through so much, but we dodged all the curve balls. Logan brings Rhett over to us handing him to Maggie. She grabs him and smiles, "I cannot wait for him to have cousins to play with just like we all have had each other. I hope they are as close as all of us." A tear runs down my face.

Collin reaches to pull Alyssa over to us and says, "Life is about to change forever."

My eyes widen and I say, "What do you mean?"

Derek walks over putting his arm around me as I look back at him and Collin.

"Oh, babies change everything," Logan chuckles.

My smile fades and everyone giggles.

"Don't worry sis, we have a pretty good village," Collin says messing with my hair, and I roll my eyes. "Please, God, I hope my child does not act like you."

Collin sticks his tongue out at me, and everyone laughs.

We may not have the house or the mementos anymore, but we have each other and that is all that matters.

Epilogue
Three years later

"Next up is a cowgirl from Maple, Georgia. Miss Megan Mapleson," the announcer says across the loudspeaker. Crackerjack prances under me at the sound of my name and I grin at the familiar feeling.

I competed at nationals and won the title two years ago. I got the title of world champion at nationals and since then it has been a whirlwind of excitement. Derek came on the rodeo road with me, and I rode in the circuit until I just could not anymore while pregnant. Nine months after finding out I was pregnant, I gave birth to a beautiful little girl, Kimber. Once she came into the world, I only do small rodeos near home, so we do not get her off her normal routine. She is already a natural around the animals and I cannot wait to see where life takes her.

"Ready boy?" I ask CJ as he rocks on his back legs ready to go. I can hear Derek at the fence with Kimber as I settle in my saddle seat.

"Go! Go!" Kimber says and I smile.

Maggie, Logan, Rhett, Collin, Alyssa, and their son Axton stand beside my little family and cheer me on.

Returning my focus to the alleyway before me, I hear the announcer say my name again and this time I give CJ the reins and power. He flies down the alleyway and to the first barrel; I sit down and grab the horn as he makes that first turn. It is perfect and clean. Pulling the horn to pull me up in between the first and second barrels, I sit back down as we get closer to the second and CJ turns with excellent force. We head to the third barrel and when I sit down again, I must hold on with my thighs because my boot comes out of my stirrup. I do not let it stop me, laying the reins on his neck, giving him all the control and just holding on for dear life.

Crossing the timer line the announcer says, "She did not come to play folks. New record! This cowgirl is not stopping anytime soon!"

I smile as I slow CJ down gradually and pat his neck. "Thank you, boy. I love you."

"Mommy go! Mommy go!" Kimber says in Derek's arms as they get closer to the horse trailer.

"You did great babe! Proud of you!" Derek says to me giving me a kiss.

"Thank you." I smile at my handsome husband and give him a kiss back. I grab Kimber from him and hold her in my arms as her arms go around my neck and give me the biggest hug.

"You are the best cowgirl ever, mommy!!" she says.

"Hey! What about me?" Maggie asks, coming around the corner of the horse trailer and Kimber giggles as Maggie tickles her.

I sit Kimber down and she runs off with her cousins and their parents while Derek helps me pack up the horse trailer.

"How did I get so lucky?" Derek asks as he wraps his arms around my waist and pulls me close to his chest. "You and our daughter are my whole world." He kisses my forehead.

I smile.

This man has gone above and beyond for me and my dreams. Thinking back to the road we started on and where we are now, it is bittersweet.

"Look mommy!!" Kimber comes running back to us with a handful of fresh flowers she must have grabbed by a nearby field. "Can we take them to my brother?"

She's almost two and half years old, and this child still amazes me. The way she speaks and her look on life, it is well beyond her age. We have always been honest with her. There are pictures of Haley in our home. I made a promise that we would never forget her, and I stand true to that. I did it for him but also for Alyssa, my new sis-in-law. We have told Kimber that she has a little brother in heaven, and we often take her with us to put fresh flowers on his grave. It's become one of her favorite things to do, picking the flowers herself.

"Yes baby! Let's get Crackerjack home and we can go!" I smile at her.

"Promise?" she asks her daddy and me.

"Promise, pumpkin," Derek says as he bends down to swoop her up in his arms.

***

We got home before it got too dark and unloaded the horse trailer, put CJ up for the night, and unhooked the truck. Kimber tells her cousins goodnight, and they all go back to their houses.

"Are you sure you want to go tonight?" Derek asks Kimber.

"Daddy, you promised," she pouts.

I chuckle, "Lord help you when she starts dating."

Derek looks sick at the thought, "Yeah about that, thinking about telling her she can't date until she's fifty."

I laugh and he helps Kimber into her car seat as we start back out of the driveway.

We reach the cemetery a little less than half an hour later and Kimber grabs the flowers she picked from the rodeo.

I let Derek get her out of her car seat and she holds both of our hands as we walk up to the tombstone where Haley and their son is buried.

Kimber lets go of our hands and she walks up to the tiny headstone, being careful to not walk over the top of the grave, and she sets the flowers down. I notice she gets close to the tombstone and whispers something but neither of us can make out what it is.

We smile as Kimber walks back over to us and grabs our hands, "Thank you for bringing me, mommy and daddy." She smiles at us.

"What did you say to your brother, Kimber?" I ask her curiously.

She smiles at me and says, "I told I loved him very much"

Tears prick my eyes, and I notice Derek wipes a tear fast, so she does not see.

I bend down and smile at my child, "You are an amazing little sister, Kimber. You are an amazing little girl. I am so proud to call you mine." I give her a big hug.

"Yep, not going to make it through the dating years," Derek says with a hoarse voice.

I laugh pulling out of mine and Kimber's hug.

"Just wait until she is driving off by herself, too." I wink and take Kimber's hand walking back to the truck.

"Ugh. I'm wounded again," Derek says holding a hand over his chest.

In that moment of our laughter, a cardinal flies down onto Haley's tombstone. We all three stop and look at it. It doesn't fly off, but it sits still and watches us.

Thank you, Haley.

I whisper as I watch it fly off and Derek leads Kimber back to our truck.

Thank you for our second chance.

Epilogue 2
Four years later

"Derek, what on earth are you doing?" I squeal as my husband picks me up over his shoulder and carries me through our yard.

"It's our first night in our new house and our daughter is staying at her cousins' tonight. I need to carry my wife across the threshold and then give her unlimited orgasms," he says while carrying me across the porch.

I giggle and let him have his way.

We started to rebuild the house where my grandparent's home was shortly after having Kimber but we did it on our own so it took longer than a construction company would have. Logan and Collin helped Derek with the hard construction work while we women decorated the inside.

Collin and Alyssa live closer now as they have built a home on his section of land that was deeded to him from our parents.

Derek and I got married last year on our land. We just had Maggie, Logan, Rhett, Alyssa, and Collin present. Collin gave me away and I know our parents and grandparents were there because a cardinal landed on my bouquet as I walked down the aisle.

He does not give me time to look around at my new home as Derek takes the stairs with me in his arms. He walks us into our master bedroom but goes past the bed and into the bathroom. The lights are dim and there are candles and rose petals all over the floor. He sits me down gently and kisses me softly.

"When did you do all of this?" I ask him, looking around.

"While you were dropping Kimber off earlier. Logan helped me," he says bashfully, and I love that I get to see this side of him now.

He really opened his whole heart up to me the day he told me I was pregnant. I still think he has nightmares about the house fire from time to time, but he will not tell me.

Seeing him become a daddy has been a blessing. He has grown so much, and we still talk about Haley often. She will always be remembered, and we have never hidden the fact that Kimber has an older brother from her. If she ever wants to take flowers to the grave, we let her. I told Haley I would never let her and their son be forgotten and I keep my promises.

Derek pulls my shirt up and over my head; he kisses my neck as he pulls me closer to him. "You know," he starts to say in between kisses, "I was thinking. We should have another baby."

I'm shocked and I look at him confused, "Are you sure?"

He smiles at me. "Kimber needs a sibling. I see how close you and Collin are. I want her to have someone like that. Lord forbid something happens to us one day, they will still have each other. Their families could be like all of ours someday. They could all run this farm together and keep the legacy going."

Tears sting my eyes as my heart rate accelerates. That is my ultimate dream. This farm to continue running through all the generations to come.

"Then let's make another baby," I tell him with a smile.

His lips crash onto mine as we walk in the shower, and he turns it on.

"You better hold on for the ride," he smirks at me.

"I think you forget how powerful my thighs are." I wink at him and that is all it takes for his lips to crash back onto mine.

Acknowledgement

To my husband, thank you for reminding me to eat and shower while i was going through writing this story. You are the light in my darkness. My second chance in a world that has always let me down. I love you!

To my ARC and Beta readers, thank you for taking time out of your busy lives to read my story and give me a chance. I cherish our friendship more than you know and I cannot wait for all the future books you will have the first opportunity to read for me. This book would not have been possible without you.

To my editor, Pat, thank you for accepting a last minute job to edit this book! I cannot wait to work with you on future projects!

To all my readers. Thank you for making LTM such a big success for me! I hope you love Megans story just as much as you have Maggies! Thank you for being here with me. I look forward to writing many more stories for you to come.

About The Author

Jessica is closer to this book than you realize. She grew up riding horses and barrel racing on her own horse. She and her sister shared a barn full of horses together in their small town. Many weekends were full of a loaded down horse trailer and a truck full of friends. This story holds dear to Jessica's heart.

Her grandparents house had a big Magnolia Tree she grew up climbing with her cousins in their yard.

Now days her and her husband love spending time on the lake, tending to their animals, and gardening.

Read more about Jessica here.
Instagram:
https://www.instagram.com/jessicawhaleybooks/
Facebook:
Jessica Whaley – Author

Did you love Megan's story?
Please leave a review on Amazon and
Goodreads!

Coming in 2025!
Collin's story will reach your kindles in
2025!

**Subscribe to Jessica's newsletter on
her website to be the first to know when it
will release!**